Noah Frye Gets
CRUSHED

Noah Frye Gets CRUSHED

MAGGIE HORNE

HARPER
An Imprint of HarperCollins*Publishers*

Library of Congress Control Number: 2023944078
ISBN 978-0-06-328519-4

Typography by Jessie Gang
24 25 26 27 28 LBC 5 4 3 2 1

First Edition

For Gabi, my forever crush.

1.

Things I Missed About Home

1. My bed
2. The dogs
3. Luna and Zoey

It takes twenty-seven minutes on the Saturday I get home from camp to realize that something's different.

It goes like this: I get home at 1:22. From 1:22 until 1:32, I'm settling in. I throw the duffel bag that smells like lake and unwashed laundry into one corner of my room and collapse onto my sweet, sweet bed. My bed that doesn't smell like all the other girls who have slept on it over the years. My bed that doesn't have one weird spring that pokes me in the middle of the night. My bed that's in my own room, away from the sound of ten other people snoring. My beautiful, perfect bed.

I'm getting off topic, but my camp bed was truly awful.

1:33 until 1:37: The doorbell rings and I launch up. When we got our phones back at the end of camp, Luna had already texted me to say she was going to run to my house the second she saw my mom's car drive down our street.

Luna pounds up the stairs and bolts into my room, leaping up into my arms. The problem is, Luna's been, like, a foot taller than me for the last year and she keeps forgetting about it. She knocks both of us over and two of our pugs spring into action to try to rescue us. Unfortunately, "rescuing" to Liza and Minnelli means a lot of snuffling and face licking.

"Hi," I say once I've crawled out from under the combined chaos of Luna's weirdly long limbs and the dogs.

1:38 until 1:42: Luna and I sit on my bed and I tell her all about camp.

"It was seriously incredible," I say. "We need to figure out how to get you out there next summer. I know Zoey's gonna be doing her theater thing, but—"

"Ooh, Zoey!" Luna lights up before I even have time to tell her about the best part of camp. "I texted her when I saw your mom's car. She said she was just getting back, but she'd be here as soon as she could."

1:43 until 1:47:

"I'm sorry you were stuck here all summer," I tell Luna. "Did you manage to have any fun between, y'know, crying endlessly about the fact that your very best friend had abandoned you?"

"Yeah, it was tough not having Zoey here," Luna says, and I shove a pillow over her face until she taps out.

Luna pushes me over and we both laugh. "But seriously," she says. "It wasn't so bad here. In fact . . ."

"I have news."

Luna and I jump up from the bed and rush over to hug Zoey. Thankfully, Luna remembers her height and, instead of jumping at Zoey, she picks her up and swings her around instead. With all three of us back in one big clump, everything feels right again. I made friends at camp who I love, but nothing beats the smell of Zoey's coconut shampoo and the softness of Luna's favorite shirt. I don't fit anywhere the way I fit into us.

Zoey usually has stories to tell us. She's what our moms call *dramatic* and what we call *fun*. My sister once told me that she's pretty sure Zoey's going to get us on TV one day, but she isn't sure yet if it'll be for a good reason.

"You have your audience," I say, and Zoey just nods like *yeah, obviously.*

"So," she says. "Theater camp."

"Theater camp," Luna agrees.

"We did *13: The Musical*," Zoey says, and I think Luna and I are supposed to know what that is, but we both just look at each other and shrug. Zoey doesn't even notice. When she gets into a story, there's pretty much no stopping her.

"I got to be Lucy."

I think that's supposed to mean something. I look at Luna, but she's no help. She's looking at me with the same expression.

"Congratulations?" I try.

"No!" Zoey says. "Well, yes. Thank you. It was awesome, obviously. But don't you get what that means?"

"I really want to say yes," Luna says. "But that would be a lie."

Zoey rolls her eyes at us. "Lucy's the mean girl in the show. She tries to steal a girl's boyfriend. Which means she *kisses* a girl's boyfriend."

3

1:48. Minute twenty-seven.

Luna gets it before I do.

"Oh my god," she says. Zoey grins hugely and nods, and Luna repeats herself.

"Oh my god!"

The two of them hug, twirling each other around. It isn't until their second rotation that I actually realize what Zoey just said.

"Wait, so you kissed a guy?" I ask.

Zoey laughs. "I kissed literally the cutest guy in the whole camp every day for two weeks."

"Oh my *god*," Luna says, yet again. I prickle, just a bit. Can't she say anything else?

But then she *does* say something else.

"We'll have to compare notes."

"What do you mean, compare notes?" Zoey demands. She drags Luna back to my bed and the two of them flop down on either side of me. I grin along with both of them, but there's a sinking feeling in my stomach I'm having trouble ignoring.

"So y'know Blake?" Luna asks.

Do I *know* Blake? Blake who lives across the street? Blake who's hung out with us since we were all little kids? Blake who ate too much ice cream cake at my last birthday party and threw up in a kiddie pool? *Blake?*

"*Blake?*" I ask in shock. Maybe it's a little rude, but, like . . . *Blake?*

"Hey!" Luna laughs. "While you two were off having your

4

best summers ever, I got bored. Blake asked if I wanted to help him out stuffing flyers for his paper route one night. We were alone in his garage, and . . . yup."

I know that *and . . . yup* means that they kissed, but there's some part of my brain that can't fathom it. The last time we talked this much about kissing boys, it was because we were watching reality TV in Zoey's basement and this couple was making out so sloppily we couldn't stop laughing at them. It feels like we're watching that again, but now I'm the only one laughing. I'm sure Zoey and Luna weren't that slobbery and weird when they had their first kisses, but it still feels off. Just a little bit wrong.

But I can't exactly tell them that.

"What do you mean, *yup*?" Zoey reaches over me to smack Luna on the arm. "I'm going to need a heck of a lot more detail than *yup*. Are you guys still talking?"

Are Luna and Blake still *talking*? They were giving each other piggyback rides when I left for camp—I should hope they've exchanged a word or two since then.

Out of the three of us, Luna's always been the shy one. I kind of figured that, in terms of order of first kisses, it would be Zoey, me, then Luna.

I guess I missed the memo.

Luna nods. "Like, all the time. The other day he showed me a bunch of new clothes he got for school, and I said I liked this jacket he got, and he was like *you can wear it if you ask nicely.*"

"Oh my god," Zoey says, yet again.

I guess that means something, and, logically, I guess that means something good, but I don't really see the connection. In fact, it kind of grosses me out that Blake thinks it's cute to talk to Luna like that. What does he mean, *if you ask nicely?* Ew.

"Y'know, at camp, I met—"

"What are you going to do?" Zoey asks, like Luna's performing open-heart surgery. I don't think she even realizes that she just cut me off, but that doesn't make it less annoying.

"What is there *to* do?" I ask, trying to elbow back into the conversation. I attempt a laugh, but it just comes out awkwardly. I never feel awkward around Luna and Zoey.

Zoey looks at me as if I just asked whether she wanted to bungee jump off my roof.

"You're kidding, right?" she asks. When I don't say anything, she rolls her eyes at me. It's fond, like I'm a cute little kid. I think I would have preferred it if she'd just been outright mean to me. "There's so much to discuss with this! Lu, are you gonna wear his coat?"

"Not right away," Luna says. She doesn't miss a beat and I peer at her to try to see what's changed about her that hasn't changed about me. "I think maybe I'll wait until school starts. Like, maybe during lunch at some point?"

"Just don't wait too long," Zoey says. "You don't want him to lose interest."

"Hey!" Luna laughs. "Who says I'm so easy to get over?"

"That's the attitude I like to see!"

6

"Guess what?" I ask, trying to raise my voice enough to be heard over the two of them.

"What?" Luna asks, smiling at me like she's just remembered that I'm in the room.

Zoey gasps. "*Don't* tell me we went three for three this summer!"

I don't really know what happens. When I look back on all of this, later, I study this exact moment over and over again, trying to figure out what I was thinking.

I think it's this: Zoey looks so excited. Luna looks *so* excited. Both of them are finally paying attention to me like I've been trying to get them to since they came into my room. Sure, they didn't seem to care about my *actual* news, but it feels so good to be back here with them, finally waiting to hear what I have to say, that the next thing just kind of . . . slips out.

"Not *yet*," I say. I don't know where it comes from; suddenly, my voice sounds just like theirs. That weird, teasing, *I have a very important and grown-up secret* voice.

Zoey lets out a feral screech and launches herself at me, grabbing me by the shoulders.

"*Who?*" she demands. "One of those science camp nerds actually had the guts to kiss you?"

Okay, a few reasons why I don't like that:

1. What would be the problem with a science camp nerd? I'm a science camp nerd.

2. Who says this nonexistent science camp nerd had to have kissed *me*? I could have kissed *him*. I don't need

to be waiting around for some science camp nerd.

3. It wasn't even technically a science camp, okay? We did a ton of other stuff.

"No," I say, digging myself even further into this hole. Zoey might be onto something with her theater stuff; something about having everyone's eyes on you makes you want to keep it up as long as possible. "I've just been talking to someone."

"Someone we know?" Luna asks.

"Maybe," I say.

Thanks, me. Really helpful.

Luna and Zoey both scream again, demanding I tell them who it is.

"It's not Blake, is it?" Luna asks.

I try to make my face seem neutral, even though the idea of kissing Blake kind of makes me want to gag.

"Definitely not," I say, and Luna looks instantly relieved.

"Are you going to tell us who?" Zoey asks.

Crap. I hadn't thought that through.

"I'll tell you if I have any news to share," I say, hoping that makes me sound cool and aloof and not way in over my head, the way I actually am.

Thankfully, the temptation to keep talking about their *real* first kisses is too powerful for Luna and Zoey to resist, so they get right back into their boy talk. I hear way more than I ever needed to know about Blake and the Cutest Guy at Zoey's Theater Camp (honestly, I don't think I even catch his name).

It's not that they're ignoring me on purpose. I get that. But that doesn't really make it feel any better when I start talking and the two of them start laughing at something else.

"Ugh," Luna says eventually, looking down at her phone. "My mom wants me home."

"Gross," Zoey says. I try to make my face look like hers, but in reality I feel a little lighter at the idea of being left alone. That's *really* not how I normally feel around Luna and Zoey, but I can also usually keep up a conversation with them, too.

"I'll walk with you," Zoey says, and she and Luna hug me goodbye. I hug them both limply back.

"We're *gonna* figure out who it is, by the way," Luna tells me just before she leaves.

"You can't hide your *secret love* forever," Zoey adds.

"Good luck," I say, and I close my door just a little too firmly behind them. (They know their way around my house almost better than they know their own houses; I'm sure they can make it to the front door okay.) Once they're gone, I let out a big breath and lean my forehead against my door.

I usually never want to be alone when Zoey and Luna are around. My house is full of noise, 100 percent of the time. The dogs running around, little nails scraping against our wood floors. My sister is usually playing music too loudly, or else she's with her boyfriend, laughing like she's going to pee her pants. When my parents are home, downstairs is all dad rock and saw-dust and the live-edge wood tables my mom makes. It can be hard to find a place that just feels like mine. I love hiding out alone in my room with all that chaos going on out there, but

Zoey and Luna make me feel calm the same way putting on headphones while my mom's using a chainsaw in the backyard does.

Today, though, I stand in the middle of my empty room for a second. I look around, sizing it up like some kind of natural disaster just occurred.

"Why did I *do that*?" I ask no one in particular.

The only response is a little pug sneeze from outside my door.

2.

Best Frozen Yogurt Accompaniments

1. Cookie dough
2. Brownie pieces
3. Your older sister butting out of your life

Nothing ever stays quiet for very long in my house.

I've just decided to start unpacking after Zoey and Luna go home (and by unpacking, I mean taking everything out of my suitcase and shoving it all into my laundry basket) when I hear Brighton's voice outside my door. That's pretty normal—our walls are thin and Brighton is loud—but she sounds particularly grumpy.

"Simon! Simon, no. Stop, Simon. Drop it. Drop it, Simon. Simon! Chicken? Do you want chicken? I'll give you chicken if you drop it, Simon!"

I open the door to find my sister staring down a pug who has one of Brighton's socks in his mouth. It doesn't take me very long to figure out the problem.

"That's Garfunkel," I tell her. "And he's allergic to poultry."

Simon only has one eye, and his brother, Garfunkel, also only has one eye, but Simon has the right and Garfunkel has the left. The dog in front of us only has a left eye. Therefore: Garfunkel.

11

Brighton narrows just one eye, like she's trying very hard not to snap at me.

"What kind of dog is allergic to chicken?"

I point down at Garfunkel.

"Garfunkel."

Both of my sister's eyes narrow at me this time.

I raise my hands in front of my chest. "Don't shoot the messenger. Plus, he knows you aren't good for it. You can't just bribe him with treats to get him to behave. That's not sustainable."

"Okay, Dr. Dolittle," Brighton says. "You get him to drop it, then."

Sometimes when Brighton calls me that, she means it in a good way, like *my little sister is an animal genius who's gonna be the world's greatest vet.* I don't think this is one of those times.

"Drop it, Garf," I say. I try to give him my sternest look, and eventually he gives Brighton her sock back. I think I see him roll his remaining eye at me before he trots off.

We have six pugs. Normally, when I tell people that, I have to quickly add *but we're normal, I swear.* Basically, when my parents first met, they each had an elderly, medically fragile pug. My mom's was named Freddie, like Freddie Mercury, and my dad's was named Bowie, like David Bowie. Both pugs were missing a leg. Soon after, my parents realized they loved rescuing disaster pugs, naming pugs after twentieth-century icons, and each other.

"Anyway," Brighton says, glaring down the hall at Garf's curly tail, "post-camp catch-up mall date? I can help you find something cool to wear for the first day of seventh grade."

I look down at myself. I haven't changed out of my camp clothes, but I don't see much wrong with my tie-dyed shirt and bike shorts. Besides, we both know I don't have something-cool-for-the-first-day-of-seventh-grade money.

"My clothes are already cool."

Brighton considers this. "I don't agree, but I respect the confidence."

I stick my tongue out at her and she does the same. We're frozen in that standoff for a while before Brighton finally breaks.

"Fine," she laughs. "Come to the mall with me and I'll buy you frozen yogurt."

I open my mouth to ask a question, but Brighton holds up a finger in front of my face.

"*Yes,* you have to change before we go."

Hmph.

"So," Brighton says an hour later around a mouthful of pineapple-raspberry swirl. She swallows, then continues, "Best summer ever? Friends for life? *Et cetera, et cetera?*"

"Pretty much." I shrug. "I actually—"

Brighton doesn't let me finish the same way Zoey and Luna hadn't. That's starting to get old.

"Speaking of friends for life," Brighton says, "did I hear Zoey and Luna talking about *kissing boys* earlier?"

"What, were you standing with your ear pressed to the door?" I ask, a little sourly. If I'd known this was all Brighton wanted to talk about, I would have negotiated for lunch, too.

Oh god, and what if she heard my lie? The *last* thing I need is for Brighton to be constantly bugging me about some guy who doesn't even exist. I think she's been waiting for me to *discover boys* for, like, five years.

Brighton rolls her eyes. "We share a wall, in case your magical camp experience made you forget the layout of your own home. And anyway, Zoey isn't exactly a quiet kid. I hear everything she says whether I want to or not."

I stir more cookie crumbs into my chocolate fro-yo. Suddenly, I don't really want to look at Brighton.

She always says that we have a Sister Bond that means no one rats each other out, but I can never be a hundred percent sure. It would be horrible to have to sit through a conversation with my parents about boys, but it would be even *more* embarrassing to have to admit that there's nothing to talk about during that conversation.

"How's Marcus?" I ask, half to change the subject and half because I actually like my sister's boyfriend. They've been together for almost an entire year, which is way longer than the other two boyfriends she's had. I think she thinks that they'll be together forever if they can make it past a year. Maybe they will. Clearly I'm no expert.

Predictably, Brighton's eyes light up when I say his name. She makes it too easy sometimes. But before Brighton can launch into a twenty-minute lovesick rant about how perfect Marcus is and all the dream dates they had when I was away at camp, I hear my name being called from behind me.

"Noah?"

I turn around and find myself grinning almost as widely as Brighton was a minute ago.

"Jessa!" I exclaim, and then feel silly. She knows her own name, I don't need to go and scream it in the middle of the food court.

"Brighton," Brighton provides helpfully. She smiles at Jessa and waves, then looks at me, waiting to be introduced.

Brighton isn't used to not knowing people. We look almost the same, except Brighton A) got my mom's bright, impossibly green eyes instead of our dad's brown eyes like me, B) has swishy, perfect, copper hair whereas our aunt Jennifer once called my hair *dishwater blond*, which, thanks, and C) Brighton already did the whole puberty thing. From what I've gathered, high school is going *very* well for her. She's probably more surprised that Jessa doesn't know who *she* is.

"This is my friend Jessa from camp," I explain to Brighton now, gesturing at Jessa.

"And as of Tuesday, friend from school," Jessa continues.

There's my too-big grin again. I've been trying to tell everyone I've spoken to since I got home about Jessa, but no one's seemed to have the time. If you ask me, the fact that we're going to have a new kid *and* the fact that the new kid is Jessa, who is *the best* and already my friend, is way bigger news than Zoey kissing some guy at theater camp. I mean, at a minimum, it's bigger news than Luna kissing *Blake.*

(Blake. I still can't believe that.)

Jessa and I met on the first day of camp when she helped me find my cabin—she'd been going to camp for a couple of years and knew the place upside down and inside out. We hung out every single day and one night I asked if she was excited to go home.

"Not really," she had said. "I used to live nearby, but just before camp started, my family moved, like, four hours away for my mom's job."

The whole summer had been amazing, but that was the most perfect moment of the entire thing. *Four hours away,* I'd thought. *I live four hours away.*

It didn't take Jessa and me very long to figure out that Jessa's new town was my town, and that Jessa's new school was my school. I'd been so excited to tell Luna and Zoey yesterday—my camp best friend and my real-life best friends could all meet and become one super-mega best friend. The *dream.*

Brighton claps excitedly, snapping me out of my fantasy in which Luna, Zoey, Jessa, and I travel the world together and none of us kiss any boys.

"That's so fun!" she says. She's so excited that Jessa takes a step back, and I blush a little. Brighton can be kind of intense if you don't know to expect it. She claims it's the result of always having to yell to be heard over the sound of six pugs breathing all at once.

16

"Why didn't you *tell me*?" Brighton asks me now. She gestures at me with her spoon, which launches little raspberry frozen yogurt flecks across the table and onto my shirt, but it's black so I don't care too much.

"I've been *trying*!" I exclaim. When Brighton picked me up from camp, she was too full of stories about everything I'd missed here for me to even get a word in. She had to update me on every vet appointment, every cool house Mom took her to, every little thing Marcus had said to her.

Actually, it was mostly about Marcus. I guess no one wants to hear about me having a new friend when there are boys to discuss.

"Well, welcome to Middletown," Brighton says to Jessa. "We have . . . uh, not much. But you probably guessed that when you had to drive forty-five minutes to get to the mall."

"We might be getting a movie theater soon," I argue. I don't need Brighton telling Jessa that Middletown sucks right away! She can figure it out in her own time.

"I checked that out while you were away," Brighton says, pointing her spoon at me. "Just a rumor."

Ugh.

"It's not that bad!" Jessa says. "I mean, my mom *loves*—oh, there's my aunt."

A tall, blond woman waves at us from where she's standing on the edge of the food court, and Jessa waves back. If Jessa hadn't said she was her aunt, I would have guessed she was Jessa's mom. They have the same ski-slope nose and bright blue eyes, but Jessa's blond hair is a few shades lighter. I haven't seen either of Jessa's parents yet, but it's clear the genetics are strong *somewhere*.

Before I can tell her not to, Brighton's waving her over. Jessa's aunt smiles, looking a bit surprised, and makes her way over to our table.

"Hi, Noah!" Jessa's aunt says. I blush a little. I already know that Jessa and her aunt are close, and that she lives in Middletown too. She came to pick Jessa up from camp, and I'd met her for half a second, but I didn't think I was memorable enough for her to recognize me. Maybe Jessa's been just as excited to tell people about me as I've been to tell people about her.

"Is this your mom?" Jessa's aunt asks, eyeing Brighton uncertainly.

I try to hide my laugh, but it doesn't go very well. Brighton gets confused for my mom *all the time* and it drives her crazy. She always waves her hand in the air and is like, *Yeah, definitely, I had you when I was four years old. It's been hard being the world's youngest mother!*

"Big sister," Brighton says. She's still trying to make a good impression, thank god, so at least she also smiles.

"That makes more sense," Jessa's aunt laughs warmly. "I was going to say, if you're Noah's mom I need to ask you about your skin-care routine!"

Oh god. I cross my fingers under the table that Jessa's aunt doesn't actually ask Brighton about her skin-care routine. We'd be here all day.

"We can drive Jessa home, if you guys want to hang out,"

Brighton says, half to me and half to Jessa's aunt. My stomach flips, I'm so excited at that idea. But Jessa's aunt grimaces.

"Any other day I'd say yes," she says. "But we're operating on a strict deal today."

"I was allowed to go to the mall for a first-day-of-school outfit if I spent the rest of the day unpacking my room," Jessa explains.

"The stuff you brought home from camp *alone* is going to take ages to put away," her aunt jokes.

I grin before I can help it. Half of that stuff is stuff Jessa and I made together, bracelets and painted rocks and things that shouldn't matter, but do to us. I'm glad she brought home as much as I did.

"Next time," Jessa promises, and I grin. "I'll see you on Tuesday, Noah! I'll text you what I'm wearing so you can tell me if I'm gonna look like a clown."

I sincerely doubt anyone is going to think Jessa looks like a clown, but I laugh and nod all the same.

I watch Jessa and her aunt leave, carrying their bags and laughing with each other, and then something starts to feel wrong. I bite my bottom lip for a second.

"So, like . . ." I say to Brighton. "I don't have something-cool-to-wear-for-the-first-day-of-seventh-grade money. But maybe I could borrow something you don't want to wear anymore?"

Brighton's entire face lights up.

"I have *so many* ideas."

3.

The Best Smells in an Animal Shelter

1. Puppy breath
2. The lavender disinfectant we clean the cat cages with
3. Fancy dog food (don't judge me)

Sunday mornings are sacred.

On Sunday mornings, I don't care about Zoey's camp boyfriend or Luna having a ridiculous Summer of Love with *Blake* or the fact that I might have implied that I've been having some kind of full-on affair with some guy all summer. I don't even have to think about the fact that Marcus is coming over tonight, which means I'll have to watch Brighton get all flirty and embarrassing over her boyfriend.

There's a lot of giggling. I'm not a fan.

I don't need to worry about anything except for my routine on Sunday mornings. On Sunday mornings, I'm in control of my own destiny.

At least until it gets too cold and I need my parents or Brighton to drive me places, anyway. And, sure, that happens pretty quickly when you live in Canada, but still. Between the months of May and September, I'm in control of my own destiny.

The next day, my first full day home from camp, I wake

up *way* before anyone else and put on my current favorite outfit (bike shorts and camp top, and I don't care what you think about it, *Brighton)*. I creep downstairs and toast an everything bagel and then eat it without anything on it. My mom calls me an animal when she sees me doing that normally, but my mom is asleep and it's Sunday morning, so I can do what I want. I put my hair in a tight bun right on the top of my head, and then finally, *finally,* I get my bike out of the garage and pedal off into the day.

It only takes ten minutes to get to the animal shelter, but I enjoy each one. Last year, when my parents first let me go there by myself, I felt like a baby that someone had accidentally let out of the house. If anyone walked by, I'd assume they were thinking, *What is this child doing out of the house unsupervised?* And I spent the entire bike ride feeling anxious.

Now, the ride to the shelter is one of the best parts of my Sunday ritual. Once I turn out of our subdivision and head onto Main Street, my shoulders relax. My chest unlocks. It's the only time I think I get why the people who come here for those silent retreats do it. The streets are practically empty this early and I can take big, deep breaths here, where no one's watching and no one expects me to be anything. It's almost like how I imagine being an adult will feel. Like I'm in charge of myself.

Middletown looks more or less the same today as it did back in June, the last time I did this trip before I left for camp. The late-summer haze is settling in, making everything feel humid and misty, but the breeze off the lake, just out of sight at the bottom of Main Street, keeps it comfortable. All the tourist shops that close on the offseason are opening, people selling shirts that say stuff like *Life is better at the lake* and *Officially on cottage time* that, for some reason, the tourists who rent the perfect cottages along the rocky lakeshore actually buy.

The shelter isn't on Main Street, but it's just down the road. Turn left at the florist, three doors down, there's the squat gray building that doesn't look at all like the land where dreams come true, even though it absolutely is. I lock up my bike in front of the shelter and bang on the door until Lydia comes to let me in.

I love Lydia. She's way older than me but maybe younger than my parents (once people pass the age of twenty, but before they get *really* wrinkly, they all kind of look the same and it's hard to tell). She dresses like me except she's an adult with really cool short green hair—she's too old for her parents to tell her she has to *think her hair choices through*. Lydia's been in charge of the Middletown Animal Shelter for as long as I've been volunteering here (three years, which, by the way, makes me the longest-serving volunteer. Just saying).

"Good morning!" I say once Lydia finally comes to the door and unlocks it for me. The shelter doesn't officially open until nine a.m. on Sundays, and the weekends are our biggest days for adoptions, so I'm here two hours early.

"Oh, I miss being that chirpy at seven in the morning," Lydia says, cupping a hand to my face. I scrunch up my nose and she laughs, dropping her hand and turning to walk to the reception desk. I skip along after her and sit on the edge of the desk when she sits in the big spinny office chair.

"How was camp?" she asks.

Ugh. *Finally*. Lydia isn't the type of person to speak over me when I try to tell her good news.

"*So* good," I say.

"What did I tell you? You had a good time, and we're right here waiting for you."

The last Sunday I was here was the week before I left for camp, and I knew I'd miss the shelter so much that I actually thought about not even going. Tears were shed. It was a whole thing.

"The *coolest thing* happened, too," I say. "I made a friend there and then it turns out she's *moving here* and going to my school."

"Sounds like destiny," Lydia says with a wink. She's one of the only people I know who can actually pull off a wink.

"What are we doing today?" I ask. I'm *more than ready* to see all the animals again.

Lydia puts on this weird evil voice and says, "The same thing we do every night, Pinky."

"If that's a reference to something, I'm too young to understand it."

Lydia puts a hand to her chest like I stabbed her and I laugh.

"Will I ruin your good mood if I tell you litter boxes need cleaning?"

As if. *Nothing* ruins my good mood on Sundays. When I'm

23

a vet, I'm going to be dealing with way worse than a few litter boxes. Besides, I can start in the kitten room. Kittens could never put a person in a bad mood.

"Can I visit Hank first?" I ask. I try to give Lydia my best puppy-eyes face, but she just laughs me off.

"I would never stand in the way of true love," she says, which means yes.

Hank is a two-year-old pit bull who's lived in the shelter for the last year and a half, which is *wild* because he's also the sweetest dog in the universe, but no one wants him because people are afraid of pit bulls. Whenever Lydia tries to show him to a family, they either refuse to meet him or say he looks too scary to have around their kids.

On my last shift before I left for camp, I fell asleep while I was reading to him (studies have shown it makes shelter dogs happier!) and when I woke up he had crawled into my lap and was snoring in my ear. But sure, random PTA mom, tell me more about how *dangerous* he is.

I would really love it if Hank found a home, but the one good part of him still living in the shelter is the fact that I get to hang out with him every weekend. I've begged my parents to let me take him home at least once a month since he got here, but we're apparently *filled to the brim with pugs* and don't have the room or the money for him.

Hank's tail starts wagging like crazy when he sees me, and soon his whole body is wiggling around too. He play-bows to me.

"Uh-uh!" I say. I hold up my hand and we stare each other down until he sits. "Good boy!"

I give him all the treats in my pocket. Hank and I have been working on not jumping up when he gets excited. I feel like it doesn't help his image.

Hank and I snuggle for a little while (he very patiently lets me squish his perfect face for a bit and everything), but eventually I know Lydia's going to come in and tell me that I *do* actually have to do my job.

"I'll see you later, okay?" I say. Hank smiles, because that's kind of all Hank does. He's the best boy in the world.

I finish saying my goodbyes to Hank and walk down the hall to let myself into the kitten room, which is pretty quiet because I guess kittens are like human babies and they sleep a lot. I stand by the little nest Lydia made for the latest batch of kittens and watch them sleep for a while. It's so cute it almost makes me want to cry, but that's nothing new for the kitten room.

Once I finally break myself away from the newborns, I get to work. During the week, Lydia cleans litter boxes by scooping poop and clumped-up pee from the box and then adding fresh litter, but when I'm here I like to give the cats something extra special. I dump out the litter from all the boxes and then get to work scrubbing and cleaning the insides. I figure no one wants a dirty bathroom, right?

There are ten litter boxes in this room, and I can usually get all of them done in an hour, but today I'm slower than usual.

While I'm scrubbing and pouring fresh litter and, okay, yeah, taking the occasional kitten snuggle break, I let my mind wander. Luna and Zoey both tried to volunteer with me a couple of times, but they never got into it. Zoey insists that a star such as herself shouldn't be dealing with another animal's poop, and Luna was too freaked out by the rodent room. Secretly, I was kind of happy. I liked having my own thing.

But after how they were yesterday, it makes me think. They barely tried to enjoy themselves here. They barely bothered to listen to me, until I made up that garbage about talking to a boy. It's not the best feeling.

I get so distracted by that extremely depressing thought that by the time I'm finishing up the last litter box, Lydia's knocking on the kitten room window. She points toward the front of the shelter—our signal that we're about to open up. I rush through the last litter box (sorry, kittens) and scurry up front to meet her.

"Who do we have today?" I ask.

Basically anyone can come into the shelter and ask to adopt an animal, but that doesn't mean we're just giving away animals to whoever wants them. During the week, Lydia does all kinds of interviews, paperwork, and home visits, to make sure that the people interested in adopting are actually going to give the animals nice lives. The people who pass all of her tests can come in on weekends and meet everyone. If they find a match, they can go home with them that day.

Told you Sundays are the best day ever.

"Just two families," Lydia says, looking down at her

clipboard. "One this morning and another in the afternoon. Could you do me a favor and file those forms on the desk? A lot of people adopted cats this week."

I roll my eyes, but I don't really mean it. Lydia *hates* paperwork. She says it's a construct of The Man, which is kind of funny because, since she always makes me do it instead, for me it's a construct of The Woman. But I don't mind—I like opening up the big filing cabinet and knowing that every piece of paper inside it represents an animal getting to go to their forever home.

The front door to the shelter opens when I'm ducked behind the desk trying to convince the sticky bottom drawer of the filing cabinet to open. I hear a few people talking to Lydia—it's probably the morning family, which is good, because Lydia appreciates punctuality. The voices sound vaguely familiar, but Middletown is small enough that everyone around my parents' age sounds familiar. I hear them say they're looking for a family dog, and my ears perk up. Dog adoptions are the most fun because the dogs actually seem to get that they're going somewhere new and good. There's an 80 percent chance that I'll cry, but in a nice way.

I pop my head up from under the desk. Everyone here knows everyone else, so I don't know why I'm surprised to recognize the person standing in front of me, but it's still a little strange to see someone you've only ever seen at school out in the real world.

Archie Jacobson. The only things I really know about him

are that he's never been mean to me or my friends, but he doesn't usually hang out with Blake and the rest of the boys who tend to hang out with me and Luna and Zoey. Honestly, though, the last thing I want right now is to be around someone who hangs out with Blake, so this is a welcome change.

It's slightly embarrassing to have to do my whole at-work spiel in front of someone I know, but I figure that grown-ups do it all the time, and they never seem to feel awkward about it. I decide to square my shoulders and go for a fake-it-till-you-make-it approach.

"Hi!" I say to Archie's parents. "I'm Noah. Do you guys want to go meet the dogs?"

4.

Best Genres of Online Videos

1. Dogs being adopted
2. Dogs being adopted
3. Dogs. Being. Adopted.

I'm a little worried that Archie's not going to want to say anything to me. Sometimes boys get weird like that (or they have ever since we got to middle school, anyway)—they're happy to be your friend in school, but outside of school it's like you're an alien to them.

But Archie grins at me, so I grin back, and after Lydia hands me their file, I lead his family down to the end of the hall where the dog room is.

"Do you two know each other?" Archie's mom asks once we're walking. "You guys look about the same age."

I squirm a little. Parents never seem to understand that just because two people are the same age, that doesn't mean they're best friends. If I had a nickel for every time my mom pointed out one of the most annoying boys in my school and said, *Well, he looks just adorable*, I'd be able to pay to adopt Hank myself.

"We go to school together," Archie says, even though that's kind of obvious. There's only one middle school here.

"I think we had English together last year," I say, even though I know we had English together last year. I just don't want Archie to think that I think about him too often, which is a little ridiculous seeing as I definitely forgot he existed over the summer.

"And you volunteer here?" Archie's mom asks.

"Yup!" I chirp. "Since fourth grade. Lydia had to invent a whole new kind of form for my parents to sign because I was so young."

Archie's dad says, "Archie could learn a thing or two from you, I think."

Archie and I both laugh awkwardly because, like, how do parents ever expect us to respond to stuff like that?

"So what kind of dog are you looking for?" I ask when we get to the door of the dog room. The dog room is really two rooms—there's a waiting room full of toys and beanbag chairs, and then the bigger back room is where the dogs live. When people are coming to adopt, Lydia and I ask them questions about what kind of dog they'd like to have and then we bring dogs through one at a time to meet them.

"We told Archie he could have a dog when he turned thirteen," Archie's dad says. "And then my wife decided she couldn't wait any longer."

"I'm so excited!" Archie's mom says, clasping her hands together. "I grew up with dogs. It's been so weird not having a dog these last few years!"

The Jacobson's file has a bunch of information from their

application, interview, and home visit, so once we're all in the waiting room, I take a second to read through it. Lots of dog experience, big backyard, no other pets or little kids—that's what Lydia calls a grand slam.

There's always someone I think about whenever we get a grand slam. Hank deserves a grand slam.

I eye up the Jacobsons carefully. I've seen them around town, of course, but this is the first time I've really spoken to them. They seem nice enough. Archie's mom seems super excited about dogs in general.

"How do you guys feel about, uh . . . pit bulls?"

I mutter the last part. I'm too used to people looking at me like I've just asked them if they'd like to adopt a fire-breathing dragon who's also a serial killer. One time a man even called Lydia into the room to yell at her for *leaving this little girl alone with dangerous dogs*.

Though honestly, that was a pretty good day. I love when Lydia yells at people.

Archie's mom gasps at my question, and I wince immediately.

"You have a pit bull in there?" she asks quietly. She even points at the door like Hank's about to come bursting through the wall. I slouch even further until my head's right between my shoulders.

Then something even worse happens. Archie's mom starts *crying*.

I've seen some wild reactions to Hank before, but no one's actually shed tears.

31

I'm about to apologize and tell her she doesn't have to see Hank and then make Lydia deal with them for the rest of the morning, because I'm pretty sure this is above my pay grade (and I don't even get paid), but then Archie's mom laughs, wiping her tears.

"I'm sorry," she says to me. "I must seem totally ridiculous!"

I shrug. "Lots of people are afraid of pit bulls. It's okay."

"Oh," Archie scoffs. "That is *not* why she's crying, I promise."

"I had a pit bull growing up," Archie's mom says. "He was my best friend."

"She talks about him *minimum* once a week," Archie says. "There's a picture of him in our bathroom."

"That makes me sound a little weird," Archie's mom says.

"You said it, not me."

Oh my god.

I don't think I even tell the Jacobsons where I'm going, I rush into the dog room so quickly. Hank's taking a nap, but he perks up as soon as he sees me. I push away the creeping, sad feeling I'm getting and replace it with hopefulness.

"Listen up, buddy," I say to Hank in my most serious voice. I grab one of the leashes hanging up on a hook and clip it onto his collar. "This is the big show, okay? Best behavior. These people have a fully fenced backyard *and* a fireplace: it's the big leagues."

Hank blinks at me, but I think he gets it.

The Jacobsons are sitting on the beanbag chairs when I

32

walk Hank into the waiting room. Archie's mom covers her mouth with both hands.

"So this is Hank," I say. Hank sits down beside me because he's the best boy in the universe. "He's two. He's been here for a while because people are nervous about having a pit bull, but he's never done anything wrong in his entire life."

That last bit wasn't part of the little speech Lydia taught me to say, but I stand by it.

Archie's mom laughs. She stands up and I feel Hank's tail start hitting me rhythmically. It wags faster and faster the closer she gets and I bite down a smile.

"He's so beautiful," Archie's mom says. She looks like she's about to start crying all over again. She crouches down to get on Hank's level, and now his tail is a total blur.

"Good boy," I say down at him. He looks up at me for a second with his big Hank smile, and then goes right back to smiling at Archie's mom. She reaches a hand out and Hank can't take it anymore—he stands up and immediately tries to put both paws on her shoulders.

"Hank!" I scold him, but Archie's mom waves me off.

"He's good," she says. "He's perfect."

It feels *so* good to hear someone else say that for a change.

I pass Hank's leash off to Archie's mom, and she walks him over to Archie and his dad. They already look like a family, and my heart swells to see Hank fitting in.

"He knows sit, lie down, and roll over," I say. "We're work-ing on stay, and every so often, if he's in the right mood, he'll do a fist bump. Basically, you hold out your fist and ask for one, and he'll boop it with his nose."

"I bet you will!" Archie's mom says down at Hank. "Because you're such a good boy!"

Hank's tail looks like it's about to fall off.

"Fist bump?" Archie tries, and Hank immediately leaps up. Thank goodness; I didn't want to have falsely advertised Hank's tricks.

"Do you guys want to see any other dogs?" I ask. I cross my fingers behind my back in the hope that they'll say no. I'm sure there are plenty of other dogs here that would be perfect for the Jacobsons, but I think the Jacobsons are the only people who are perfect for Hank.

Archie's mom and dad look at each other for a second, having one of those silent parent conversations.

"Absolutely not," Archie says. Both of his parents laugh, but neither of them disagrees with him.

"How's it going—oh."

Lydia's at the door to check on us, and I know her face probably looks a lot like mine right now. I think I might even see a tear or two in the corners of her eyes.

"I don't want to break this up," she says. "I was just coming in to see if you were having any luck in here."

"I think we've had excellent luck today," Archie's dad says.

I just barely resist jumping up and down.

"How about grown-ups follow me for some paperwork?" Lydia suggests. "Noah, I'll let you give Archie the crash course in all things Hank."

Everyone else leaves the room and it hits me that Hank's actually getting adopted. He's *actually* going to leave the shelter and go to his forever home. He's not going to be here on Sunday mornings anymore.

"Are you okay?" Archie asks, and I realize in horror that I'm crying.

I wipe at my eyes as quickly as I can and try to stuff everything down.

"Sorry," I say. "Hank's just become my buddy, y'know? I know I'm being dramatic."

"That's not dramatic," Archie says. He sits back down on one of the beanbags and I sit on the one beside him. Hank comes to sit between us and puts his head in my lap. I can't look him in the eye or I'll cry again.

"I mean, I know we aren't best friends or anything, but we *do* know each other," Archie says. "You can always just come and visit him."

I hadn't thought about it like that. At least Hank's going home with someone I kind of know. I might get to see him again, and if I do, the next time I see him, he'll be living in a real house!

"And I can send you pictures, if you give me your number," Archie says, and then makes a face. "Sorry, that sounded weird. I'm not trying to be weird. Just trying to provide Hank content."

I laugh a little, wetly, but I'm glad that Archie acknowledged that it's kind of weird for us to suddenly have this connection. Nothing against Archie or anything, but ever since *giving someone your number* became an actual thing people at school talked about, the idea of it's felt strange. I plug my number into Archie's phone and he smiles easily at me.

"Maybe you could send some when you guys get home?" I ask. I hate how little and pathetic my voice sounds, but it really wouldn't be that weird if Archie sent me a picture of Hank today. Or maybe a couple of pictures. Or maybe five to ten pictures per day, forever.

"Oh my god, obviously." Archie pretends to roll his eyes. "You're, like, a Hank expert. You're not gonna be able to get rid of us, you'll have to be on call twenty-four seven."

I know he's just trying to make me feel better, but it works, so I don't call him out on it.

Archie and I hang out with Hank for a little while longer—now that I know I'll still get to see him, it's easier for me to show Archie how to scratch the specific spot behind Hank's left ear that he loves. Eventually Lydia's face appears at the door again, and Archie, Hank, and I make our way to the front of the shelter.

Archie's mom freaks out again when she sees Hank. She immediately crouches down to meet him and starts baby-talking him. If she were my mom, I'd be super embarrassed, but because she's not my mom, and because I think Hank deserves someone who's that obsessed with him, I just think it's nice.

Everyone's so excited about Hank going home—Lydia makes each adopted dog pose with a sign that says how many days they've lived in the shelter so she can post the pictures online—that I don't even notice there's someone else in the shelter until she stands up from one of the reception chairs by the door.

"Do you want a ride or what?" Brighton asks. Her hair's all messy, but it just makes her look cool instead of like a cave-woman, which is what I look like if I let my hair go wild like that.

My brow furrows. "You don't usually come get me until later."

The agreement my parents and I have is that I'm allowed to bike to the shelter in the mornings, but once Brighton's awake in the afternoon, she picks me up. On a good day, I can usually sweet-talk her into *at least* a convenience store Popsicle, so it's an arrangement that works well for me. Or at least, it does when Brighton follows protocol and picks me up at the right time.

"Sorry, kid," Lydia says. "I called her."

"What?" I demand, possibly a bit too loudly, because Hank's ears go flat.

"It's good to take a bit of time for yourself when one of your favorites gets adopted," Lydia explains. "I've got everything under control here—you take it easy and I'll see you bright and early next week."

"You're cleaning the litter boxes next week," I mutter.

Lydia laughs. She has this massive, booming laugh that always makes me smile even when I'm trying not to.

"Deal," she says. She even lets me shake on it.

I don't want to leave early, but I *especially* don't want to say goodbye to Hank. Even though I know it's not a real goodbye, it's still the last time I'll see him in the shelter. I'll never come here on a Sunday morning and get sloppy Hank kisses all over my face again.

Archie walks Hank over to me and I smile gratefully at him. I take a long time giving Hank a big hug (and, okay, possibly shedding a few tears into his fur), ignoring the fact that Brighton's started dramatically tapping her foot behind me.

"Love you, buddy," I whisper. "Have the best life."

"Check your phone," Archie says once I stand up.

I try to wipe my eyes without it being too obvious and then pull my phone out of my pocket. Archie's sent me three pictures of Hank and me saying goodbye that he must have just taken.

"Thank you," I say to him. "Seriously."

Archie nods, and I let Brighton lead me out of the shelter. She helps me stuff my bike into the back of dad's minivan and doesn't say anything until we're pulling out of the parking lot.

"Who was that guy?" she asks.

I know exactly where she's going with this, and it sours the whole morning I just had.

"Hank," I say. "He's a two-year-old pit bull."

Brighton rolls her eyes at me. "Who was that *human* guy?"

Brighton knows pretty much everyone in Middletown within a two-year age radius, which means Archie doesn't quite make the cut.

I roll my eyes back. "Archie. His family just adopted Hank."

"He was cute!" Brighton says.

I scowl. "You're right," I say. "Hank is very cute."

5.

Best-Case Scenarios: First Day of School

1. Jessa is in my class
2. I receive thirty thousand photos of Hank throughout the day
3. Luna and Zoey agree that Jessa's the Coolest Person in the World and we all ride off into the friend sunset together

Normally, it's terrifying to get to school on the first day and have to pray to the back-to-school gods that Luna and Zoey and I will share classes. In elementary school, it was different—teachers thought we were well-behaved enough to put in the same class without worrying we'd spend all our time talking to each other. But middle school is a whole other story. Last year we had the same homeroom English class, but for the first time ever, we didn't have a single other class with all three of us. Luna and Zoey had gym together without me. Luna and I had geography together. *None of us* were in the same science class. It was a mess.

When the three of us walk into school on Tuesday morning, though, I'm surprisingly calm. I figure with Jessa around, I have an even better shot at having homeroom with someone I know.

Like that same magic that I'm pretty sure got Jessa here in the first place, when I see *Mr. Cross, room 204* on my timetable and *Mrs. Romanevsky, room 207* on Luna and Zoey's timetables, I'm totally calm. There are only two seventh-grade homerooms, and for some reason, I just know that Jessa's going to be in mine. Mr. Cross teaches geography, so Jessa and I are definitely going to be able to talk to each other more than Luna and Zoey, who have homeroom math. The thought makes me shudder.

"This is awful," Zoey says. She even drags her hands down her face for dramatic effect.

"We'll tell you everything at lunch," Luna assures me.

It's not that I'm happy that Zoey and Luna aren't in my homeroom. I'll miss having class with them first thing in the morning and then going our separate ways after we've updated each other on everything that's happened overnight. That's what we did last year, and it always made me feel like I was starting the day with two people totally on my team. But I'm not as completely freaked out as I would have been without Jessa around. Obviously, in a dream world, all four of us would be in the same homeroom, but for now I kind of like keeping Jessa to myself. Just for a couple more hours.

Just as I suspected, just like magic, when I make my way into Mr. Cross's room (after two lengthy hugs from Luna and Zoey outside the door, like they were my parents dropping me off on the first day of kindergarten), Jessa's already at her desk. Three rows back, near the classroom door. A perfect spot. She grins at me when she sees me and I grin back, rushing over.

"No assigned seating," she says. "I checked."

I make myself comfortable at the desk beside Jessa, carefully unpacking my binder and pencil case that managed to survive last year in relatively good shape. Jessa has new stuff laid out in front of her—the shiny plastic cover on her binder reflects the fluorescent lights overhead.

"So," Jessa says. "Just you? You have those best friends, right? Luna and Zoey? Or did you make them up to sound cool at camp?"

For a second I think she's serious, but then I see the way she's trying to hide a smile and we both laugh.

"My invisible friends Luna and Zoey," I agree. "They're sitting right beside me, can't you see them?"

The classroom's still pretty empty, kids just starting to file in while Mr. Cross gives out smiles and high-fives, welcoming everyone to his class at the front of the room. I have plenty of time to get Jessa up to speed.

"They're in the other seventh-grade homeroom," I say.

Jessa grimaces. "That sucks, I'm sorry."

I shrug. "It's no big deal, really! I'm pretty sure Luna's . . . whatever-he-is is in that class, so she'll be thrilled."

"Her whatever-he-is?" Jessa laughs. "Is that how you say *boyfriend* here?"

"I don't know what he is. They've apparently been kissing up a storm all summer, anyway."

I'm about to say *so it's probably for the best that we don't have to witness that,* but I stop myself. Thank goodness I do because Jessa smiles.

"That's cute," she says. "They'll get to see each other every day."

41

Of *course* Jessa thinks it's cute that Luna and Blake have been kissing. She probably thinks it's nice that they're a couple or whatever they are, because that's what everyone else seems to think. Clearly I've been living under a rock. Luna and Zoey had no trouble becoming the kinds of girls who kiss boys and talk about their crushes, so why should Jessa be any different? Jessa's always seemed more mature than other people I've met my age; it's part of what makes her seem so cool and interesting. Of *course* she doesn't have any weird feelings about people our age having crushes and kissing boys. I'm sure she's never panic-lied to her friends about a fake crush. I'm sure she's *also* been kissing up a storm.

Ugh, and why did I say *kissing up a storm*? Who *says* that?

"Yeah," I agree, like an absolute fool.

Mr. Cross claps his hands to get everyone to listen to him, and I've never been more grateful for a teacher in my life.

I wasn't nervous about my homeroom situation, but I am *definitely* nervous about introducing Jessa to Luna and Zoey.

I shouldn't be nervous; it's not like I'm springing Jessa on them out of nowhere. Hey guys, meet best friend number three! I finally got the chance to bring Jessa up in our group chat on Sunday night, but something about the conversation left a funny taste in my mouth.

I'd painstakingly crafted the perfect introduction message.

I told Luna and Zoey that Jessa was from the town near camp, that she'd moved to Middletown this summer after her mom got a job nearby. I told them that Jessa was the fastest swimmer at camp and that she played basketball at her old school and she doesn't have any pets or siblings but she has a lot of cousins who she loves. Every little detail about Jessa that I thought they'd find interesting, I told them.

And Zoey said: Cool! We can have lunch with her or something then

And Luna said: Yeah 😊

It's not like I expected them to fall at Jessa's feet and start talking nonstop about how much they already loved her and how excited they were to hang out with her, but I thought they might have given me *something* to work with. But no, as soon as both of them had given Jessa that weak little stamp of approval, it was right back to them dissecting a conversation Luna and Blake had the day before down to the syllable.

My name is popping up less and less in our group chat. I can't quite tell if they've noticed it yet.

"Do you guys get a lot of new kids?" Jessa asks as we walk into the lunchroom. I haven't seen her since homeroom, but between now and then she seems to have shrunk a little.

I laugh before I can stop myself. "Basically none. We've all been in the same little groups pretty much since before we were potty trained."

Jessa bites her lip, and I realize why that was probably not the correct thing to say.

"But that just makes you really cool and special!" I rush to say. "I promise, they're going to love you. And if they don't, then they're clearly displaying a *severe* lack of judgment and it would be in my best interest to ditch them for you."

I'm pretty sure Jessa doesn't believe me, and I try not to think too hard about what would happen if Luna and Zoey *don't* like her after all. But Jessa smiles and says *thanks* in a tiny voice and I try to throw away all of those bad thoughts. There's no *way* anyone in the *world* could not like Jessa.

Luna and Zoey are waiting at a table for us, and when we get there they're already talking full tilt about something that must have happened during homeroom. I don't have any other classes with any of them in the morning, but this afternoon Zoey and I have French together and I have science with Jessa and Luna. Jessa, Luna, *and* Zoey have English together without me, which sucks so much I can't think about it too hard, but it's still a little better than last year. Either way, I have a feeling we'll be using these lunches to catch up on the morning's events.

"You're here!" Zoey says when she sees Jessa and me. At first I'm happy she's making such an effort, but then I realize Zoey has a story to tell. She's looking for an audience.

"This is Jessa," I say, before Zoey can continue. Sometimes talking to Zoey is like a Wild West duel: you have to draw first if you want any chance at survival.

"Hey." Jessa waves, a little awkwardly, and I'm suddenly relieved that she's feeling nervous too. I'm glad she thinks this is a big enough deal to be anxious about. I'd kind of been worried that if things didn't go well with Luna and Zoey, Jessa would realize she's cool enough to ditch us and find other friends.

Zoey and Luna say their hellos as Jessa and I slip onto the bench attached to the table.

"Happy first day!" Luna chirps at Jessa, and Jessa smiles back. Okay, good. This is working. This is okay.

"Thanks," she says.

"Were you nervous this morning?" Zoey asks. She doesn't have much of a filter, and normally, I love her for it.

Jessa shrugs. "I think I would have been a lot more nervous if I didn't know that Noah goes here. Even just knowing one person made it easier."

"Especially when that one person's as perfect as Noah!" Zoey says, and I forgive her instantly for being in story mode when we got here.

"Oh my god," Zoey says, looking down at her phone. "Oh my god."

She's getting a FaceTime call from someone whose name I can't quite make out on her screen, but there are three heart emoji beside it. That can only mean bad things.

"I can't believe he's calling me at school," Zoey says, but she flips her hair like *of course* whoever "he" is, he should be calling her at school.

"Let me see him!" Luna leans over.

"Oh my god, you should answer it," Zoey cackles and tosses her phone to Luna.

"Hiiiiiii," Luna says, leaning into the phone and then

laughing like someone's just told the funniest joke in history when the guy on the phone goes, "Uhh, hi? Can I talk to Zoey?"

"What do you mean?" Luna asks. "I *am* Zoey!"

That makes Zoey's laugh go from giggle to full-on shriek, and she grabs the phone out of Luna's hands.

Zoey makes a face at the guy on the screen I've never seen before. She kind of looks like she smells something bad, but she enjoys it.

"Why are you calling me?" she asks. I don't hear what the guy says, but she laughs and rolls her eyes. "Oh my god, you're so stupid. Wait, are those your friends? Spin me around! Hi everyone! Okay bring me back please! Hi! Stop being stupid, I'll call you after school. Maybe. Ugh."

She hangs up, and I feel like I'm watching a nature documentary. Except there's no old British man with a beautifully soothing voice to tell me what's going on.

"Well, we *obviously* have to talk about that after school," Luna says. She's grinning like she understood all of that. Did I go to the wrong camp? Was there a class I missed over the summer?

"You're all coming over tonight, right?" Luna asks. She waits for me and Zoey to nod and then turns to Jessa.

Jessa smiles at being invited, which makes me smile.

"Sure," she says. "I need to ask my mom, but she's so worried about me making friends that she's going to freak out over this anyway."

At least there's that. At least Luna and Zoey are welcoming

Jessa into our little group. That's what I've wanted to see ever since Jessa and I found out we'd be going to the same school this year.

Maybe there's still a weird feeling in the pit of my stomach that's been there since Zoey's boy called her. Maybe it doesn't feel like it's going away anytime soon. That's nobody's business but my own.

6.

Things I Hate

1. Reality TV
2. Reality TV about interior design
3. Reality TV about interior design that makes the houses look a hundred times worse than they started

I've been going to Luna's house for as long as I can remember because for as long as I can remember, we've lived just down the street from each other. Before I even started kindergarten, my mom told me that the new family a few doors down had a little girl my age, and my mom took it upon herself to set up a play-date with her. The rest is history, I guess. I'd know every inch of Luna's house no matter what changed in my life. You could blindfold me and spin me around and set me loose and I'd still be able to grab snacks from her fridge before heading upstairs to her room.

Which is why I try not to see it as a bad omen when I bump into a table in her front hall when I arrive after school.

"Sorry," Luna says. She grabs my arm to steady me. "That's new."

This whole "everything's new" thing is starting to feel pretty old.

Luna leads Zoey, Jessa, and me upstairs to her room, where all of us sit on the fake sheepskin rug in the middle of her floor. Luna pounces on Zoey the second the door's shut.

"Okay, tell me everything."

I didn't think there would be much to tell—we were all there in the cafeteria, and we all witnessed the half conversation Zoey had with her camp boy (I still have no idea what this guy's name is). But apparently, that was the kind of thinking reserved for the old version of us, before Zoey and Luna learned Boy Language.

"So he was with pretty much all of his friends, I think."

Luna narrows her eyes. "Boys or girls?"

"Mostly boys, a couple of girls. Is that bad, do you think? Should I be worried?"

"I mean, I wouldn't love it." Luna purses her lips and Zoey looks crushed.

"I'd take it as a good sign," Jessa pipes up. "If there were no girls, I'd worry that either he was rude to girls so none of them wanted to be around him, or that he was trying to hide something. I think he was probably just being himself."

Zoey seems to like that much more, so she immediately decides that has to be what's happening.

"That's good," she says. "That makes sense. Thanks."

"Now," Luna says, giving me a look that I can only describe as *sinister*. "We had a question for *you*, Noah."

I don't really feel like Luna, Zoey, and I are on the same page right now, but that doesn't mean I don't still know them really, really well. I still know all of Zoey's favorite musicals (that's actually way more impressive than it sounds because she changes the list monthly) and the names of the girls on Luna's league soccer team who go to different schools, even though I've never met them in my life.

Crucially, that means I also know when they're being weird, and they're definitely being weird. As soon as Luna speaks, she and Zoey sit down on the edge of Luna's bed together, hands folded neatly on their laps. They look like they're about to lead a very important business meeting.

"Noah Frye," Zoey says in her Stage Voice. "We need to discuss a matter of greatest importance."

"Yes," I say immediately. "That was the question, right? Do I want to order pizza? Yes."

"Your Halloween party this year has to be the best one ever," Luna blurts out.

"I had a *whole thing* prepared!" Zoey whines.

"You always have a whole thing prepared," Luna says. "Sometimes we need to get to the point in under an hour."

"Sorry," I say. "Why does my Halloween party need to be so amazing?"

My parents are obsessed with Halloween. Preparations generally begin in September, and it all ends with a candy-coated party on the night itself. Usually, parents hang out together and all of my friends hang out in the basement. My dad cooks enough food for the whole neighborhood and we fall into a food coma after a couple of hours. It's the best.

"Things are *different* this year," Zoey says, still looking extremely serious. "I think we should invite boys."

We should *invite boys*? Blake's been to every one of these parties since I was old enough to invite friends. Half the boys in our class live within walking distance of my house, and most of them at least drop by for my dad's cooking.

"Am I missing something?" I ask. "Have we not been inviting boys the whole time?"

I'm smiling like I'm joking around, but . . . what?

"There's a difference between inviting boys as friends and Inviting Boys," Luna says so sagely I can practically hear her dramatic capitalization. "If we're Inviting Boys, then the whole party's vibe changes."

The idea of the Halloween party's vibe changing does *not* sound like fun to me. When I look at Luna and Zoey, though, they both look so happy and excited about this whole thing that I already know there's not much I can do.

"Change away," I say, smiling tightly. "You now have full creative control over the *vibe*."

Luna squeals. "I'm so glad you said that, because I've already made a list of new things we should add to the party."

Zoey grabs Luna's phone and starts scrolling through the list.

"Oh, *excellent* work," she says. "Can we go over this tonight? Like, research and start planning? We can divide the list and then report back."

"Obviously," Luna says.

"New things like what?" I ask.

"New decorations, new lighting schemes, new food, new costumes . . ." Luna reads through the list on her phone. "It's a pretty exhaustive list."

Right. So now we have to change everything about this party just because boys—sorry, I mean Boys—are going to be there?

"What about you, Jessa?" Luna asks. "Any boys from your old school we should be inviting?"

I don't want to sound too negative here, but I seriously doubt *anyone* from Jessa's old school is going to drive four hours to come to my Halloween party, different vibes or not.

Jessa blushes. "Definitely not."

"But you're blushing," Zoey says.

I squirm uncomfortably. I didn't want Jessa to start hanging out with us just to start getting interrogated by Zoey and Luna. I've always hated that *but you're blushing* thing that people do. I'm a sympathy blusher and it never works out well for me.

"And now Noah's blushing!" Luna points out. Ugh. "You must know something then, Noah."

Jessa's face has gone purple-red, but she collects herself.

"Seriously, I wasn't interested in any of the boys at my old school. They were pretty immature."

Ooh, excellently played. Now Luna and Zoey are going to think Jessa's extra cool, above all of the middle school drama and the middle school boys. I'm proud of her for holding her own.

"Oh," Zoey says. "Okay! Well, then maybe you can give us a clue about the boy Noah's been texting all summer."

Crap. Crap, crap, crap. I thought I'd gotten away with this whole fake crush thing—I figured that once school started again, Luna and Zoey would figure out that they had more stuff going on in their lives than boys, and they'd forget I ever said anything. I hadn't thought they'd ask Jessa about it.

"You've been texting a boy all summer?" Jessa asks. I can't quite read the look on her face; mostly confused, definitely, but she might also be a little hurt that I didn't tell her about this mystery boy before.

"You didn't even tell Jessa?" Zoey asks. "We should send you to best friend jail."

For about five seconds, I panic. I have *no idea* what magic words I should say to make this situation disappear, and the longer I go without saying anything, the weirder the whole thing seems.

I think back to everything I've ever heard Brighton say that made me roll my eyes. Every time I've been forced to sit through a reality dating show with my mom. And I try to channel all of that energy into a response that seems aloof, yet reasonable.

"I just don't want to say anything until I know whether something's there."

"Noah Frye!" Zoey says, delighted. "I didn't know you had it in you!"

At first, it feels kind of good to surprise Zoey like that. It's fun to make her think a different way about me. But then something about *I didn't know you had it in you* makes me a little embarrassed. Does that mean she's been thinking I'm missing something?

While I'm contemplating whether my best friends have secretly been thinking I'm a loser, Luna turns the TV in her room on for background noise. Unfortunately, a pretty woman with bright orange hair and freckles, wearing pink coveralls and grinning into the camera, appears immediately. Everyone but Jessa groans.

"Booooooo," Luna, Zoey, and I call in unison.

Rural Refresh is this show that started filming in Middletown two years ago. Pink Coveralls, whose real name is Brylee James, decided to storm into town one day and start renovating all the beautiful old houses. And when I say "renovating," I mean "destroying."

She paints bricks white. She paints trim white. There was even an episode where she painted one-hundred-year-old hardwood floors white. She says stuff like, *The concept for this space is modern farmhouse meets seventies cool.*

Like, what does that even *mean*? I hate her.

Unfortunately, I think Luna and Zoey and I are the only ones who hate her. Middletown's always been one of those places that gets really busy in the summer, when everyone from the city goes to their cottages by the lake and fills up all the shops and restaurants on Main Street. But up until two years ago, winters were almost silent, except for the sound of snowmobiles racing along the frozen water. I've always thought Middletown was pretty year-round, but it took Brylee James aggressively tearing down interior walls to make other people believe it. Ever since her show started airing, more and more people from the city have started moving here, working from home and opening up yoga studios and cooing over how *quaint* Middletown is.

"Why boo?" Jessa asks. "I thought people loved this show."

Aw man, there it is. I knew not *everything* about Jessa could be perfect.

"We can forgive you for liking *Rural Refresh* because you weren't here to see what Middletown looked like before," Luna says. "You don't even know what you're missing."

My parents always say they moved here because they fell in love with the houses—my mom because of the ornate wood-work on their fronts (which, she always reminds me, is called gingerbread) and my dad because each house was a little bit different and had *its own energy*. Since *Rural Refresh* was successful enough for a second season, every time I see another one of those big old houses with a coat of white paint slapped on the brick, it kind of makes me want to cry. Like Brylee James is telling them they aren't good enough as they are.

"I don't know," Jessa says, looking off to the side. "I think she seems nice."

Luna pretends to gag, which, okay, might be a bit much, but I agree anyway. I nudge Jessa's foot with my own so that she knows we aren't making fun of *her*, just Brylee James.

"*Brylee James* is not nice," I say. "If she was nice, she'd leave us all alone and go take her design business to some city somewhere."

"She could open up a store where she only sells cans of white paint and beige macramé wall hangings," Zoey says.

"That's not fair," Luna says. "You forgot about the single blue pillow she puts on the couch at the last second *for a pop of color.*"

The three of us laugh so hard that it doesn't take very long for Jessa to start laughing with us. That's good, because making fun of *Rural Refresh* has become one of our favorite sleepover activities.

"Plus, whose name is *Brylee*?" I demand. "That's not a name. That's just a sound."

Jessa scoffs. "All names are just sounds."

"Whoa," Zoey mutters to herself, looking like Jessa just blew her mind.

"We're not even that *rural*," Luna says. "We might be getting a movie theater soon."

I don't have it in me to break that one to her.

We watch the intro to *Rural Refresh* for a little bit. It's maybe the worst part of the entire show. Brylee James walks down a street that's supposed to be a street in Middletown, except actually I recognize all of the houses she passes and they're nowhere near each other. She stops every so often, pretending to examine a house. Then, she puts on this ridiculous TV smile, snaps her fingers, and the house gets turned into one of her boring monsters. She does it three times, all with houses I've walked by my whole life and don't recognize anymore. Luna, Zoey, and I boo each time she does it, and that helps a little.

Eventually, though, it gets tiring—there are only so many jokes you can make about such a boring subject—and Zoey switches the TV off. Luna and Zoey stretch out, arguing absently for a while about whether Luna's going to paint Zoey's toenails like she apparently said she would in homeroom. Without thinking about it, I lie down on my back with my head on Jessa's outstretched legs.

I've done this a million times with Luna and Zoey, and they've done it to me, too, but I haven't done it with Jessa and I suddenly feel self-conscious. I didn't ask if I could barge into her personal space like this. Maybe she's not the kind of person that would be comfortable with that.

"Sorry," I say. I start getting up, but Jessa shakes her head.

"You're good," she says. She smiles down at me and I lie back, a pleased little hum in my throat at how well Jessa fits in with us.

"So," Jessa says. "We sort of met your guy at lunch, Zoey. What about Luna's?"

Blake sat with us at lunch almost every day last year, but suddenly today he was sitting with all his guy friends on the other side of the cafeteria. Zoey grins as Luna covers her face. I just manage to resist rolling my eyes. Why pretend like you don't want to talk about Blake when Luna's *clearly* been dying for someone to ask her about him?

"His name's Blake," Luna says. "He's *really* nice."

"And a good kisser, apparently!" Zoey interjects, and Luna swats her, but they're both laughing.

"So are you guys dating?" Jessa asks.

"I don't really know," Luna says, deflating a little. "I think we need to talk about that."

I keep quiet while Zoey and Jessa interrogate Luna. All I keep thinking is, *Really? Blake? Blake who told us girls weren't smart when we were in the second grade and I kicked him in the shin? Blake who cries at dog food commercials? Him?*

If this were last year, things would be different. I don't always have the easiest time being heard. At home, if someone's not operating a power tool or playing music or barking, they're laughing or talking super loudly. Don't get me wrong, it's nice to live in a house where everyone's always laughing and we all like talking to each other, but it means that if you're like me and you don't always want to be loud, there's always someone else around to be loud for you. And that usually means that, even though I know my family loves me, I also know they don't always hear me.

It used to be different with my friends. If this sleepover were happening last year, we'd be doing what we've done every other time we've hung out since the beginning: talk. About everything. About what we want to do and where we want to go and who we want to be. And if I was quiet, or if it took me a second to figure out what I wanted to say, Luna and Zoey would wait. They would listen. Sure, Zoey can get loud and dramatic, but never when it counts. Neither of them would ever make me feel like I needed to be different for them to listen to me.

Except now *they're* different, and I don't know how I fit into it.

Jessa doesn't seem to notice that I'm not speaking. Actually, Luna and Zoey don't, either. When Blake or Zoey's camp boy or any of the other boys who are suddenly cute instead of annoying get brought up, no one seems to notice much about me at all.

I look up at Jessa, laughing at something Zoey just said. She looks completely at ease with everything—with this conversation, with this place, with my friends. I'd been so worried that she'd feel like the odd one out with us.

So why do *I* feel like that?

7.

Things That Make Me Feel Better

1. Ice cream
2. The pugs
3. A good, solid plan

It takes me until next Sunday to figure it out.

I realize that I've been conducting experiments without even realizing it. This cannot stand. I'm a woman of science: I know better than to start experiments without documenting my observations!

It started the day I got back from camp; I told Luna and Zoey I'd been texting a guy, and they believed me immediately. Now, whenever I feel like they're starting to drift away from me, I've realized all I need to do is bring up this mystery boy and they're all over me again, trying to figure out who he is. The more mystery boy gets brought up, the closer to normal things seem.

(I mean, besides the fact that we're dissecting interactions with boys in the first place, but at least this way Luna and Zoey talk to me like I'm their equal and not like someone's little sister that we're babysitting.)

So, I need to make this experiment official.

Assessing Friendship Elasticity in Courtship Habits of Twelve-Year-Old Juveniles

(Or: Will my friends still want to hang out with me now that they have boyfriends?)

Observation: Major changes in friendship dynamics have been observed for the last two weeks. A request to change the "vibe" of our Halloween party has been made.

Question: If I joined in with the boy talk, could things feel normal again?

Hypothesis: Presenting my friends with a crush and enthusiastic participation in the Halloween party will bring back our friendship, allowing me to change our friendship group back to the way it was from within.

Method: . . . I'm working on it

So far, the Halloween party is the perfect thing to bring up when I don't know what to say—it's boy adjacent enough to get through to them, but not so boy focused that I don't know what to say. But I know I can't keep that up forever, and I'm going to need to bring forward a new phase to the experiment.

I've looked at this from every possible angle, and I can finally admit to myself what I've been dreading all week: if I'm going to give this experiment the fair shot it deserves, I'm going to need a boy.

To tell my friends I have a crush on him, I mean. I don't need to, like, keep one in my basement.

Unfortunately, I don't think the perfect boy for this experiment is going to fall from the sky, so I'll need to spend the next week observing candidates and trying to decide who it might be.

I'm not looking forward to it, but at least I can temporarily forget about the whole thing on Sunday morning. I step into the shelter and take a deep breath.

And then my shoulders slump without my permission.

"It's just as depressing as I thought it would be without Hank."

I know I'm being dramatic—Archie sent me a couple of pictures of Hank settling in at home last week, so it's not like I haven't seen him at all—but with everything getting so weird in my life lately, even the shelter is struggling to lift my spirits. There's only one file on the desk, which means we only have one appointment today. The fact that it's a slow day seems even more depressing, like no one even wants to come and rescue an animal.

"As your boss, I'm going to have to stop you right there," Lydia says. She gestures for me to follow her and then plops herself down on her desk chair. I take the hint and sit on mine. When I first started volunteering, Lydia only had one chair up here. After she realized that I wasn't going to go anywhere, she got me my own chair to celebrate my first anniversary at the shelter.

"You're being extremely morose for a twelve-year-old kid with the world at her fingertips," she says. I can never tell if Lydia's being sarcastic or not, but she doesn't ever make me feel bad for that. A lot of times, with grown-ups, they act like you don't know what you're talking about just because you're younger than them. They make it seem like they know every-thing and if you even *try* to know something—about life, about other people, about yourself—you're just being cute. I'd love to know what happens on your twentieth birthday that apparently makes you the master of all the knowledge in the universe.

Lydia isn't like that. Even when I first started coming here as a little ten-year-old fourth grader, she always at least *pre-tended* like she was interested in what I had to say. Sometimes I think about what life would be like if I were her age, and we were grown-up friends who dyed each other's hair and rescued dogs. Seeing as I haven't quite figured out time travel yet, I just have to hope I'll have a friend like that when I grow up.

"How old were you when you had your first boyfriend?" I ask her. It's probably best to rip off the Band-Aid. Lydia's basi-cally my test for what's actually cool and what people my age just *think* is cool. Like, last year Blake was really into this app where you posted a picture of your face and then the app showed you what you'd look like as a bunch of different types of people, but Lydia went on this whole rant about online privacy and selling your face to The Government, so I didn't get it. It was definitely the right idea, too, because we all ended up having to go to an assembly about internet safety that went on for *ages*, but at least I didn't need to feel any guilt about it.

Lydia scoffs and then gives me a funny look, one eyebrow raised. She looks at me for a second longer, like she's trying to figure something out, and then her face smooths over, but she looks away.

"Uh," she says. "I think I was about nineteen."

"Nineteen!" I exclaim. "Yes, exactly. Perfect. *Perfect* boyfriend age."

"Thank you?"

"You know way more about the world when you're nineteen," I say.

Lydia laughs again. "It's so sweet that you think that."

"Well, you know more than when you're *twelve*! How many love songs talk about being nineteen? And then how many love songs talk about being *twelve*?"

"I don't think any love songs talk about being twelve," Lydia agrees. "Probably because it would be creepy."

"Exactly," I say. "It's weird."

I'm definitely pouting at this point, but Lydia's basically the only adult whose judgment I trust and who won't make me feel like a baby for thinking how I'm thinking.

"Are you having . . . boy trouble?" Lydia asks, giving me that same weird look as before.

"Ugh, no," I say. "Everyone *else* is having boy trouble, and that's somehow become a problem for me, too."

"*Oh*, okay." Lydia nods. "That makes more sense."

"What, because I'm so unappealing?" I ask sarcastically. I don't *want* any boy trouble, but that still felt like a bit of a sneak attack.

Lydia hoots, which she does when she thinks I'm being extra funny. "No, because you just . . . didn't seem like the type of kid to be worried about boys. And good for you! You've got more important stuff to worry about, right? I was like that too."

"Yeah?" I ask. I try to be casual about it, but I'm pretty sure I look slightly rabid at even the hint that Lydia also didn't care about boys in middle school.

"Definitely," she says. "And I wish that I'd had someone very cool and interesting such as myself to tell me that it doesn't matter."

It makes me feel a bit better, because talking to Lydia always makes me feel better, but it's still not quite all the way better. Lydia's already done middle school. She's a grown-up who doesn't *need* to care about whether her friends will still want to be friends with her if they have boyfriends. It's easy for her to say it doesn't matter.

I don't think I'd ever say that to Lydia, but I don't get the chance either way, because both of us are pulled out of our conversation by the door chimes letting us know someone just walked in.

As soon as I realize it's Archie, I'm narrowing my eyes at him.

"If you're here to return Hank, you can just turn around right now," I say.

"If I was here to return Hank, my mom would be here tomorrow to put *me* up for adoption."

Lydia laughs and I relax my shoulders slightly. Okay, maybe I don't need to physically fight Archie Jacobson this morning. That's probably a good thing.

"Now that we've settled that no one is being put up for adoption, what can I do for you?" Lydia asks.

Archie shuffles his feet a little awkwardly. "I was wondering if you guys needed any extra help, like on the weekends or whatever? Like what you do, Noah. I thought it looked really fun."

Ugh. Sure, it's nice when people want to help out at the shelter, but I've been volunteering long enough to know that most of the time, when a kid comes in because their parents told them to, they don't last very long. Not every shift is cuddling kittens, and even if it were, kittens poop *a lot*.

My phone starts buzzing where it's laid out on the desk in front of me. I know I'm not supposed to look at my phone when I'm talking to people, but I glance down at the screen as quickly as I can. I make out the little emoji stars we named our group chat with before I went to camp, and see a lot of exclamation points and Blake's name.

My heart sinks. I thought that maybe they were so excited about all their boy stuff just because they hadn't had time to talk about it all summer. But I guess this is just all we talk about now.

Or, I guess I should say it's all *they* talk about. They don't seem to mind so much that I'm not talking about it with them.

Lydia's voice pulls me out of my self-pity nosedive.

"It's not that we wouldn't love to have you," she says, "but we're really not that busy. I can't promise that you'd actually get to do very much work."

Archie's shoulders slump and his eyes go big like he's a cartoon character. Huh. It's nice that he actually seems to care about this. That's kind of unexpected.

The beginning of an idea is starting to unfurl in the back of my head. I decide it's best to not overthink it—or think it at all, really—and speak up.

"I could really use the help!" I say. "I mean, it's not like you have to pay us, right? What do you have to lose?"

Lydia looks at me for a few seconds. I think she's trying to size me up, so I sit up a little straighter to make it seem like I really know what I'm talking about.

"He should definitely start volunteering," I say, just to really drive it home.

Lydia still doesn't look entirely sure, but I know she doesn't have a leg to stand on here. I'm right: she doesn't need to pay us, so why *not* let another kid come scrub litter boxes?

"Welcome aboard, I guess," Lydia says.

Archie grins at me and I grin back.

Boy: acquired.

8.

People Responsible for the World's Atrocities

1. War criminals
2. People who ban books
3. Brylee James, probably

By the time I get home on Sunday, I feel a little lighter about everything.

Sure, there's a chance I'm backing myself into a corner with my experiment, but at least I have a plan now. At least I can do something about it. And if, at the end of the experiment, I have an actual boyfriend who I actually like, I guess that's something I'll be excited about too.

And anyway, Archie doesn't seem so terrible. In terms of all the boys I know, he's definitely closer to the top of the pile than the bottom. I've never seen him laugh when someone does something embarrassing in class, for one thing. His hair looks reasonably soft. As far as I can remember, I don't think I've ever thought he's smelled bad.

Plus, he *loves* Hank. He's basically all we talked about during our shift, which suited me just fine. Isn't that pretty much the only thing people like each other for, anyway? Zoey and her theater camp boy have acting stuff to bond over. Luna and Blake have . . . proximity, I guess? So Archie and I can have animals.

For the first time since school started, I'm not dreading Monday morning. I have a *plan* now, and if there's one thing I love, it's a good plan. Everything is about to go back to normal. I can tell.

I've been home from the shelter for an hour when Brighton storms her way inside. For someone who likes to pretend she hates the chaos of our house, Brighton tends to bring chaos with her wherever she goes. If she stays home for too long, she starts to act like Bonnie and Clyde when we tried to crate train them: jittery, sad, and way too loud.

"Why are you home?" I ask. Yesterday, Brighton decided that it was officially fall and she was going to dress as such, meaning that it's now way too warm outside for her outfit and she's overheating. Her face is about as red as her hair, which is sticking to her forehead, but she still looks pretty good. It's annoying.

"Nice to see you, too," she huffs. She takes off her hat and jacket and then her sweater and the button-up shirt she'd been wearing underneath the sweater, until she's just wearing a tank top. She leaves all her stuff in a pile on the stairs that she'll forget about until our parents yell at her to clean up after herself tomorrow. There's about a 60 percent chance that one of the dogs will have peed on her clothes by then, and my money's on Clyde.

"Dad texted me to come home," Brighton says. She looks around like our parents are going to pop out from behind a door and explain what's going on. When they don't, she shrugs. "I guess I beat them here."

My parents were born ages after hippies were a thing, but my dad is pretty much as close as you can get these days. My mom took over the woodworking business from my grandpa after she graduated high school, and the first person she hired was a painter named My Dad (well, he wasn't my dad yet, and his name is Edward, but still). They figured out the whole pug thing, fell in love, and started a home renovation business the year after Brighton was born.

We aren't really "family meeting" people. My parents have made it clear that they're always there for us if we need them, but my dad thinks we'll, and I quote, *bloom brighter if you can see the sun*. I think that makes a lot of sense to him, but it doesn't make much sense to me.

I know as soon as my parents step inside the house that something's wrong. Normally, they stop and say hello to each pug, investigating all six of them carefully to make sure that none of them need immediate medical attention or belly rubs. Today, though, both get inside and kick off their shoes. My mom smiles at me, but she looks tired.

"Thanks for coming home, Brighton," she says.

"Thought I'd grace you with my presence," Brighton replies.

Neither of my parents laugh at that, which is even weirder because they think me and Brighton are hilarious.

I don't remember my parents ever acting like this. They aren't themselves. Normally, the house feels alive when they come home. They make things brighter and louder and funnier and better. I don't feel any of that right now.

"Is someone dead?" I ask.

"Is someone *dying*?" Brighton asks.

My mom chuckles, so at least that's something, but then she looks sad again.

"No one's dead or dying," my dad says. He tilts his head. "I mean, *some* people are, obviously. But no one we know."

"So why are you acting like it?" Brighton demands.

My parents sit on the little green velvet love seat in our living room that no one usually ever uses. They found it at an estate sale and it's just too big to sit on by yourself and just too small to sit on with someone else. They're so squished together that my dad's leg is basically on top of my mom's.

"You two have seen what's been going on in the town over the last couple of years, right?" my mom asks.

Brighton and I look at each other. She gives me a look like *no clue* and I shrug.

"Things are changing," she continues. "When your dad and I first moved here, things were . . . quiet. It was a small town that got very busy in the summer. Now, it's a medium town that's getting busier and busier, no matter what season."

"Isn't that a good thing?" Brighton asks. "I mean, not for, like, environmental reasons, but at least for business reasons?"

"Yes and no," my dad says. "With everything going on with

71

Rural Refresh . . ." I cut him off by making a gagging sound.

"If you're telling me that you guys are going to go work for *Brylee James,* I'm never speaking to either of you ever again."

"That's not what's happening," my mom says.

Oh, man. My parents normally *love* my *Rural Refresh* smack talk. This is more serious than I thought.

"Basically, we're . . . well, *struggling* probably isn't the right word, but . . ." my dad says.

My mom's always been more direct. She says, "The market for the kind of work we do for people just isn't in demand. Our style isn't Brylee James's style, which *is* in demand."

Brighton gets it before I do. "So, what, something's wrong with the business?"

My heart sinks. My parents put everything into their business. They love it so much that it would break their hearts to have to give it up and find normal-person jobs.

"Things aren't going as well as they should be," my mom says. "We weren't prepared for something like *Rural Refresh* to happen, so it's been a bit of a struggle over the last little bit. It doesn't seem like Brylee or *Rural Refresh* are going anywhere anytime soon, so we need to figure out how to adapt."

"Is this, like, a *we're not eating name-brand cereal anymore* struggle, or a *we're moving in with grandma and grandpa* struggle?" Brighton asks.

My mom purses her lips for a second. "Somewhere between the two."

That's a worse answer than I thought it was going to be.

72

"We have savings," my dad says. "And we can sell a few of our bigger staging pieces. But a lot of people are struggling right now, and it's difficult to tell when things are going to get better."

"We hope to be back on track next year," my mom says. She puts her hand up to Brighton when she says it, and Brighton closes her mouth, question answered. "*Rural Refresh* is what's trendy right now, but Brylee James can't replicate the work that we do. There are a lot of houses, especially all those big log cabins by the lake, that need very specialized woodwork that only I can do. Brylee can only really do the decorating; I can make houses more structurally sound and secure. But until then, we're going to have to buckle down a bit. Essentials only for the next year or so."

"It'll be good to get back to basics," my dad says. He doesn't look completely convinced.

"We're going to pare down our spending," my mom says. "And we'll cut some nonessentials. We don't *really* have to feed the whole town on Halloween, right?"

Wait, what?

No. Absolutely not.

"Yes we do!" I say. I accidentally kind of yell it and everyone, including the pugs, jumps.

"Sorry," I say. "But . . . yes we do? My friends look forward to that party all year. Luna and Zoey are *so* excited about it."

"We aren't saying you can't have a party," Dad says. "Just that it won't be the same as they've been in the past. A few snacks, no new, flashy decorations. Maybe you can make your costumes this year too."

So everything Luna and Zoey have been excited about. Cool.

I've never really been the kind of kid who says stuff like, *My parents just don't get it*, but this time it's true. Their one little budget cut could ruin my entire friendship group.

Okay, I know how ridiculous that sounded, but I can't bring myself to care at the moment.

Luna and Zoey have been talking about everything they want to change at this party. I haven't been keeping very close track, but it's expensive. They want food from a specific restaurant. They want speakers. They want animatronic decorations.

It's not that they're spoiled, it's that they've never had to think like us. I mean, Luna's parents are both *doctors*. A lot of the time, they just assume no one worries about money, because they don't worry about it. This isn't the first time I've looked at my life and their lives and seen a lot of differences, but it's the first time those differences seemed like a problem.

I feel a tear running down my cheek before I fully realize I'm crying.

"Can I go upstairs?" I ask.

My dad frowns. "I think we should all probably talk about this more. We can—"

"Go ahead, Noah," Mom says. She and Dad share one of their patented parent looks where they think they're being subtle, but I can tell exactly what they're thinking.

Dad: *We need to process our emotions as a family! Every feeling should be seen and validated!*

Mom: *She's twelve.*

Dad: *Oh god, good point.*

I bolt upstairs, trying to go as fast as I possibly can because I know my parents and Brighton are going to continue talking about me and this whole awful situation and I don't want to hear any of it. I wipe roughly at my cheeks as I shove my door open. I slam it shut and flop on my bed, dropping my face into my pillow and letting myself cry for just a minute longer.

My phone buzzes. I almost don't want to check, because I wouldn't put it beyond my dad to try to text me about this, but when I see Jessa's name on the screen I start running on autopilot. I immediately unlock my phone and video call Jessa. Suddenly, there she is, smiling absently in front of her white bedroom wall.

"Oh, hey," she says when she picks up. "I was just gonna ask, do you think—wait. What's wrong?"

Even if I *wanted* to pretend like nothing was wrong, I know that I must look like a complete mess right now. There's no hiding from this, even if I'm kind of hoping that if I curl up tightly enough I'll *poof* into another dimension and I can stop worrying. About my friends leaving me behind. About some ridiculous crush on some ridiculous boy that doesn't seem to want to show up. About the fact that it feels like all of the differences between Luna and Zoey and me are about to become so big and obvious that no one is going to be able to ignore them.

"Brylee James is what's wrong," I sniffle.

Jessa arches an eyebrow. She might even look a little annoyed, which makes me feel even worse. "I mean, I know you hate her show, but that seems a *bit* dramatic."

I try to scoff, but it kind of dies in my throat and turns into a sob.

"It's not dramatic at all," I say. I explain what my parents just told us, and Jessa's eyes get wider and wider. By the time I get to the part about how they basically just killed the party, I'm crying even harder than I was before.

"Oh," Jessa says once I'm done.

"Yeah, *oh*," I reply. I don't want to keep crying, but my breath is weak and keeps hitching, and seeing the disappointment on Jessa's face makes me start up all over again.

"Okay," Jessa says. "Okay."

"Okay what?" I ask through my tears. "It's not okay."

"But we aren't going to fix it right now," she says. "You have to breathe for a second. We can fix it later."

I know that's probably not true. Like, what, am I going to start trading stocks to solve all my parents' financial woes?

"Close your eyes," Jessa says. I feel a bit ridiculous, but I do it. "Listen to me. We'll figure it out. It'll be okay. Just take a few deep breaths with me."

I do as I'm told. I think Jessa probably meant for me to open my eyes again after, but I don't. Right now, with my eyes closed and Jessa speaking quietly, it feels like I can float away from all of this. If I open my eyes, the spell she cast might be broken and I'll have to deal with it again.

"Can you just keep talking to me?" I mumble. I put my phone on my pillow beside my head and squeeze my eyes shut even more tightly while Jessa starts talking about . . . honestly, I have no idea what she talks about. All I know is her voice is soothing and it's almost like she's here with me. It doesn't take too long for it to lull me to sleep even though it's still light out.

9.

Scariest Possible Things

1. Zombies
2. History tests
3. Your friends making plans without you

Assessing Friendship Elasticity in Courtship Habits of Twelve-Year-Old Juveniles, v.2

(Or: Will my friends still want to hang out with me now that they have boyfriends?)

Observation: Major changes in friendship dynamics have been observed for the last two weeks. A request to change the "vibe" of our Halloween party has been made, and recent events have demonstrated this is impossible.

Question: If I joined in with the boy talk, could things feel normal again?

Hypothesis: Presenting my friends with a crush and enthusiastic participation in the Halloween party will bring back our friendship and teach me how to actually have a crush on a boy, thus ensuring long-term friendship stability. Plus, apparently I'm going to want a boyfriend at some point, so it would be nice to have one locked in.

Method:

1. Select target. Target should be reasonably nice, and have never used the phrase "girl books" when talking about a book with a girl protagonist and/or that is written by a woman. **Step completed.**
2. Telling friends. This should be done at a sleepover or another intimate gathering to maximize impact.
3. Forced proximity. Doing something together with the target will make him realize I'm very cool and fun and interesting.
4. Flirting. From what I understand, this is heavily insult-based and neverending.
5. Group hangs, school
6. Group hangs, outside of school
7. Kissing

It's a little embarrassing to admit, but I wrote down a hard copy of my experiment to refer back to on Sunday night. Even though I'm not exactly excited at the idea of kissing Archie, at least I managed to figure out a good target. He was way more fun to hang out with yesterday than I thought he'd be. It might have had something to do with the fact that when it's just us at the shelter, neither of us has to worry about what other people might think if they saw us hanging out.

I've been trying to psych myself up all day for Step Two of my experiment: I'm going to need to tell everyone that I have a crush on Archie. I'm hoping that the excitement of the announcement just sort of . . . erases the fact that I've already told everyone we've been talking all summer, but the idea of

Archie finding out I said that about him makes me want to dig a very deep hole and then live out the rest of my days at the bottom of it.

"We're at your house this weekend, right?" Luna asks. I take a deep breath I hope no one notices and try to school my face back into excited-about-sleepover-night Noah.

"Yeah," I say. "I asked yesterday, we're good."

Luna and Zoey nod, but when I look at Jessa to make sure she can come too, she's looking down at her lunch. Zoey and I give each other a look.

"Are you coming, Jessa?" Zoey asks.

Jessa perks up, her face going a bit red. "Oh! I, uh . . . I wasn't sure if I was invited."

I want to both smack her for thinking that and smack myself for letting her think that.

"Oh my god, of *course* you're invited!"

We do sleepovers pretty much every Saturday night, rotating houses so that we don't wear out our welcome with someone's parents too quickly. Sleepovers *used* to mean staying up extra late, convincing my parents to order pizza, and bothering the pugs. Now, apparently it means planning. I hadn't even realized that I'd forgotten to officially invite Jessa—with us, there's never a need for an invitation because we already know we're always welcome.

Luna's halfway through dividing her spreadsheet between the four of us when she cuts herself off midsentence. She's staring at something just behind me. It's extremely creepy.

"Jeez, what?" I ask. I turn around, but there's no serial killer lurking behind me. Instead, Archie's smiling, phone in hand.

"As promised," he says, holding the phone out to me. I realize what he's talking about and whip it out of his hand.

On Sunday, Archie and I got to talk enough for me to feel comfortable calling him out for not sending me *nearly* enough Hank photos. I mean, he's been there an entire week now! Just *think* of all the stuff I've probably missed!

Hank's there on the screen and seeing him almost makes me cry. Archie lets me scroll through a ton of pictures—Hank curled up on the couch, Hank curled up in front of the fireplace, a selfie of Hank and Archie squished face-to-face in bed—and I make a different squealing noise at each one.

"And this one was from last week," Archie says, reaching over me to tap into a video of Hank sitting in Archie's kitchen. I watch as the camera pans to a bowl filled with chicken, brown rice, and apple slices.

"Hank's first dinner at home!" Archie's mom's voice says from off camera. Hank can't sit still anymore and starts spinning in circles. Eventually, he can't take it and lets out a little howl.

I grab Archie by the arm.

"Look at him!" I say. "Oh my god, I love him. He's doing okay?"

"He's awesome," Archie confirms. "My mom keeps looking at him and crying. They're, like, best friends."

"Amazing," I say. I let go of his arm and we smile at each other one more time before Archie heads back to his usual table.

The high of getting to see Hank lasts approximately one second, because as soon as Archie's gone, Luna and Zoey are looking at me like I just grew a second head.

"Holy *crap*," Zoey says.

My shoulders immediately slump. "What?" I ask.

I know what. Of course I know exactly what.

"You've been talking to *Archie Jacobson* all summer!" Luna explodes. "That's your secret guy!"

I don't say anything, but that's confirmation enough as far as Luna and Zoey are concerned.

"Cancel all of our sleepover plans this week," Zoey says. "We need to figure out our *Archie plan*."

Okay, seriously, when did boys' names start being italicized?

I try to push past my annoyance at this whole situation, because Luna couldn't have given me a better opportunity if she'd tried.

I can't *quite* bring myself to actually, specifically, seriously lie, and the idea of saying *I have a crush on Archie* feels *horrible*. So I find a way around it.

"I don't need a plan," I say. "He'll like me back because I'm great."

There's a half second when everyone processes what I just said, but then both Luna and Zoey pounce on me at once.

"I *knew* it!"

"How long have you liked him?"

"Why didn't you tell us sooner?"

"Do you think he likes you back?"

"Stop, of *course* he likes her back, who *wouldn't* like Noah back?"

For a second, I kind of forget this is fake. I'm just excited because they're excited, so before I even realize what I'm doing I'm laughing and celebrating right along with them. Is this what it's been like for them since the summer? This excitement, this bond, this feeling of possibility at what the future might hold?

It's a lot. I can see why they like it.

I peek at Jessa, who's watching all of this go on with a funny look on her face.

"You like Archie?" she asks.

I squirm but try not to make it noticeable. For some reason, it feels weirder to lie about this to Jessa than it does to lie about it to Luna and Zoey.

"Yeah," I say. "He started volunteering at the shelter with me."

That isn't really a reason to have a crush on someone, but I think it sounds reasonable enough. I mean, come on. Luna told me she kissed Blake by saying *and . . . yup.*

"So what are you going to do?" Luna asks me. She looks at me the way I've seen her look at Zoey lately. Like I've leveled up, the same way they have. Like we all get it, and now we have this whole new language we can use together.

"I want to get to know him more," I say. "Before I . . . y'know, make a move."

Make a move? Oh my god, this is so embarrassing. I'm just parroting whatever garbage I've seen in teen movies. I cringe at myself internally.

Shockingly, though, that seems to have been the right thing

to say. Zoey raises her eyebrows like she's impressed with me. She leans back to look me up and down, like she's seeing me in a new light.

"I love that," she says. "Good for you, making the first move."

"Yeah," Luna agrees. "I was way too chicken to tell Blake I liked him. If he hadn't said anything we would have just gone around in circles forever."

"But seriously, Noah," Zoey says. She puts a hand on my arm from across the table. "Thank you for telling us. I was starting to get worried that you thought we were annoying with all our boy talk. I'm *so* glad you can join in now!"

I just smile, even though that makes me feel so much worse. I'd half expected them to say something like *oh thank god, now you can finally stop being boring and we can start talking to you again*. I hadn't expected Zoey to say she was worried I found boy talk annoying. Does that mean I could have just asked them to stop it and they would have? And if *that's* true, does that mean I've been wasting my time with this experiment?

No, of course not. No science is ever wasted.

A year or two ago, if you asked me, Zoey, or Luna if we liked any of the guys in our class, we'd have said, *Ew, of course not*. It's just that I would still say that, but now that's a problem somehow.

Last year, Luna, Zoey, and I would watch the couples that popped up and seemed to go away before we could even blink. We watched the flirting and the drama from afar and laughed about it all. Why would they want to be the ones we were laughing about now?

"So, question," Jessa says. *Oh no.* Now Jessa's going to get involved. Back at camp, she saw right through me, and she wasn't afraid to call me out when she did. The week I snapped at her and told her I didn't want to go swimming because swimming was stupid, she left a pad under my pillow, no questions asked. Of *course* she'll figure this out, too. I tense, bracing myself for whatever it is Jessa's about to ask.

"Why have we decided that Halloween is the holiday to go this hard for when it's just going to snow and ruin our costumes anyway?"

Luna and Zoey laugh. I try to let out the breath I'd been holding without it being too obvious. Jessa just saved my butt, and she doesn't even know it.

Something softly nudges at my foot. I startle, but no one notices because Jessa, Luna, and Zoey are all still talking to each other about how cold we're going to get trick-or-treating. I try to peek under the table without it being too obvious and see Jessa's foot touching mine. So maybe she *does* know it. She knew I needed the conversation to move away from me, and she knows as well as I do that the Halloween party is the best way to change a subject. She's apologizing for bringing it up and it almost makes me want to cry, because it feels so nice to know she has my back even when I'm lying to her and everyone else.

Jessa nudges my foot with hers again. I nudge back. The rest of lunch feels a little easier after that.

10.

Uncool Sleepover Activities

1. Weaving
2. Poetry
3. Calling boys

A weird, tight feeling stays in my throat for most of the week. When Archie smiles at me when I get to homeroom in the mornings, I keep my smile as quick and boring as possible. He doesn't approach me with photos of Hank in person again, but we've been texting more. I've had friends who were boys before, but that was Before, when everything was normal and made sense and it wasn't weird to have friends who were boys. Before, Luna and Zoey wouldn't have thought twice about seeing me talk to a boy, but now it has this whole extra *thing* attached to it. Now, any time I talk about Archie or if my friends even *think* I'm talking to Archie, it's like something about me changes. They all sit up straighter. They all listen more carefully. Even Jessa.

It's great for my hypothesis, but it's not awesome for my self-esteem.

I wish I could just be happy about finally having a friend I can bother for dog pictures, but ever since lunch on Monday I feel like I'm always having to look over my shoulder, just in case someone gets the wrong idea about me and Archie.

I'm happy to talk to Archie one-on-one about Hank and whatever else he wants to talk about as long as it's after school, through a screen—he's really into these Scandinavian teen dramas you can only find on sketchy illegal websites. So far he hasn't convinced me to watch one, but that hasn't stopped him from trying. Archie hasn't given me any kind of indication he likes me in any way but as a friend (and even then, it's not like we're suddenly this super tight-knit best-friend pair. Archie seems to think about me the same way I think about him: a pleasantly unassuming blob), but I clearly have no idea how boys work now so maybe I'm missing signs. I'd much rather speak to him with a bit of distance between us, just in case.

But I decide that I can put all of that aside for the weekend. I mean, Luna and Zoey might have changed a little over the summer, but even they would agree that nothing should ever touch sleepover night.

"Can I have the tablet in my room tonight?" I ask my dad in what I hope is my sunniest, most favorite-daughter voice possible.

He makes a face like he's devastated. "Can't you and your friends do something more engaging with your time? You could play with my old pottery wheel! You could *weave* something!"

". . . We could *weave* something?"

I can't quite hide the laugh that startles out of me.

"'Hey, guys, party at my place tonight!'" I say. "'Yeah, my dad's gonna let us use his *loom*.'"

"Well, I *was* going to let you use my loom, but after that show of blatant loom disrespect you can forget about it."

My dad actually looks a little pouty that I disrespected the art of weaving.

"I'm sorry about the loom disrespect," I say. I pause just long enough to be acceptable before adding, "Where did we land on the tablet?"

He pretends like I stabbed him in the chest, stumbling around for a couple of seconds for good measure. I let him get it out of his system.

"I will take my friends and all six dogs on one walk around the block," I offer.

He thinks about it for a second, stroking a beard he definitely doesn't have.

"Deal," he finally says. "*If* you all bring back a memory of nature with you. I *will* be asking."

I know I'm going to regret asking this question, but he leaves me no choice.

"What's a memory of nature?"

Dad shrugs. "Y'know, a cool cloud you see. The smell of rain. The particular shade of red on a leaf."

I blink at him a couple of times, waiting for him to start laughing.

"I'm gonna go get the tablet," I say.

"I'll also accept spoken-word pieces about how the approach of autumn makes you feel!" he calls after me.

A couple of hours later, after the pugs have been walked and then returned to the loving care of my parents on the living room couch, we're all wedged on an air mattress on my bedroom floor.

Jessa *loved* the pugs, thankfully. I tried to explain Simon and Garfunkel's eyes and Liza and Minnelli's missing legs (Liza's only missing one, up front, but Minnelli uses a special wheelchair) and the fact that Bonnie and Clyde have anxiety and scarf down, like, ten CBD pills a day each, but visitors tend to experience pug-information overload and I don't think anything really sticks. Honestly, sometimes even Luna and Zoey mix them up. But Jessa was still appropriately in love with them, so she was allowed to stay.

Lying between Zoey and Jessa, I can almost forget about the previous week. In fact, when it's just the four of us, lit up by the glow of the tablet that's probably set up too close to our faces, I forget about the rest of the *world*.

Luna has the reins, scrolling through different shows and movies while she and Zoey argue lazily about what we should be watching. Zoey's been into watching wedding shows lately, which means *my* new hobby is swallowing down all my reactions when she dreams about her wedding with theater camp boy.

"If you guys don't pick something soon, I'm gonna fall asleep," Jessa says. She's not lying—every so often her head slumps onto my shoulder, sitting there for a bit until she startles herself awake.

Luna and Zoey must not take Jessa seriously, because they keep arguing back and forth between the same two shows. Honestly, I don't want to watch either of them. Jessa's really warm beside me and it's making me sleepy.

Just when I start dozing comfortably, I'm jolted awake by Zoey yelping. At first, I think Luna's finally gotten sick of this argument and pinched her leg under the blanket they're sharing, but then I see that Zoey has her phone in front of her face.

"Oh my god, Liam's calling," she says.

Theater camp guy is named Liam, I guess. Huh.

"Are you gonna answer?" Luna asks. Her eyes are wide and panicked, and I have to wonder yet again whether she and Zoey are actually *enjoying* this. Everything seems so life-and-death that it must be really stressful. I can't picture myself having a good time like that.

"I don't know!" Zoey yells. "I look horrible!"

Zoey never cared about what she looked like at a sleepover before. Or ever, really.

"Oh, just answer it," Jessa says. She sounds a bit annoyed, but she smiles a bit after she says it to soften it. "If he doesn't like you just because you haven't spent hours putting makeup on or whatever, you shouldn't be wasting your time on him anyway."

Zoey considers that for a second, then nods and accepts the call.

So there's Liam. I saw him on the first day of school, but not up close, in detail like this. I try to put aside all of my feelings about the whole Zoey-leaving-us-for-boys situation and look at him objectively. Maybe I'll see what she sees in him.

Liam looks . . . like a boy. He has two eyes. A nose. His hair's kind of cool, I guess—a freshly cut fade. But is that reason enough to kiss someone?

I'll say this, at least: he seems really, really happy that Zoey answered the call. He's grinning, and it makes Zoey smile back. Suddenly, she doesn't seem so worried about what she looks like.

"Hi," Liam says. He's with a big group of people because I can hear a dull roar coming from all around him, but his voice still fills my room. Both because Zoey has her phone volume turned up all the way and because I'm pretty sure Liam's using that Theater Voice Zoey's always talking about.

"What are you doing?" Zoey asks. I think she's trying to do that thing where she pretends like she's annoyed that Liam called, but she's smiling too widely for it to be believable.

"I missed you," Liam says. Three different people make retching noises from behind him and I snort.

"Who's that?" Liam asks.

Zoey raises the phone and pans it over us—Jessa and Luna wave, and I try to, but it feels like my wave comes too late and I just feel awkward.

"Noah thinks we're gross," Zoey says to Liam. I flush. I hadn't realized I was being so obvious.

"I don't think you're gross," I say. Jessa laughs quietly beside me and I can feel my face burn hotter.

"Me neither," Liam says to Zoey. His eyes are all big and lovey.

"Okay, now I think you're a little gross," I say.

Zoey laughs, rolling over onto her stomach so she can focus in on Liam. I glance over at Jessa, who looks at me and rolls her eyes good-naturedly at Zoey. I instantly feel so much better—I don't *want* to be the weird grump telling Zoey and her boyfriend-or-whatever-he-is that they're gross! I don't even know if *gross* is the right word for it. It's more like uncomfortable or awkward or off. Brighton sometimes says that I feel things so hard that I make everyone else feel it too. She mostly says that when we're arguing over pizza toppings, but she might have a point. I feel so weird at the idea of Luna and Zoey dating that I can't imagine that they *wouldn't* also feel weird about it.

"I bet you wouldn't think it was gross if *Archie* was calling." Zoey tears herself away from Liam just long enough to thrill me with her astounding wit.

I hate how she says his name. *Aaaaarchie.* Why does everything have to have this double meaning?

"Probably not," I say. "Because Archie has a dog who's *definitely* more interesting than this conversation."

All of Liam's friends start laughing and talking at once, *oooh* and *burn* and *daaaaamn!* The smile freezes on Zoey's face for just long enough for me to know that I hurt her feelings. Luna cackles, because Luna never thinks anything is mean. In elementary school, we had to tell her that Gillian wasn't actually joking when she said she wasn't going to invite Luna to her birthday party and it became A Whole Thing.

I didn't *mean* to be mean. It just came out.

Luna rolls over onto her front as well so she can poke her head into Zoey's conversation. The two of them swat at each other and make Liam and whoever else is on the other side of the screen laugh, and I let my head loll to the other side to look at Jessa. Except she's leaning up on an elbow, already looking at me. My face gets hotter than it did when Zoey called me out.

Jessa scrunches up her mouth, raising an eyebrow at me: universal silent language for *you okay?*

I flash her a tight, closed-mouth smile that I know doesn't convince her of anything, but it's not like I'm going to say *hey, I don't have a crush on anyone and I don't think I even understand how anyone* could *have a crush on any of the boys at our school but I think that might also make me an immature baby, thoughts?* right here in front of everyone.

Jessa looks at me for another long moment. The longer her eyes are on me, the squirmier and more awkward I feel. Eventually, though, she calls Luna's name, pulling her out of her conversation with Liam and Zoey.

"Are we doing that Halloween party thing?" Jessa asks. "I've already started researching costumes, and if you've made me do homework for nothing, I will *not* be happy."

"*Ooh,*" Zoey says. I guess Liam isn't *so* intoxicating that Zoey can't still overhear conversations happening around her. That's a bit of a relief. "I have to go."

"Do you have to?" Liam asks. He makes this cartoonish sad-puppy face and Zoey actually almost squeals.

"Don't be cute!" she says. "You're the one who interrupted

girls' night. We have important work to do."

Girls' night. How did I miss the moment when us hanging out, same as always, had a whole new name?

Zoey hangs up the call, and all of us get organized with our research. Zoey, Luna, and Jessa all brought their own tablets, and I'm trying not to think about how the one I'm using belongs to my whole family to share.

Once Luna and Zoey are deep into their research, I glance over at Jessa. She's not looking at me this time; her hair's falling out of its loose bun in little blond wisps, lit up by the glow of her screen. I nudge her thigh with my knee twice: *thank you.* She doesn't look at me, but she smiles down at her screen. Her leg presses into my knee three more times: *you're welcome.*

11.

Things I Don't Like

1. Change
2. Irresponsible pet owners
3. Pickles

Brighton kicks down my door early in the morning and we all groan in unison, stuffing our heads under pillows and each other's arms.

My first thought is *oh no, I didn't warn Jessa.* Luna and Zoey are used to this: I can faintly hear rain hitting my bedroom window, which means my parents must have asked Brighton to drive me to the shelter. She takes a sick amount of pleasure in these early morning wake-up calls.. It may have slipped my mind to tell Jessa about the risk of being kicked out of my house pre–seven a.m. today.

Luna and Zoey sit up, rolling kinks out of their shoulders from sleeping on an air mattress that gradually deflated through the night. Jessa's still squeezing her eyes shut, like she can will this away, and I laugh.

"I'm sorry," I whisper. "I forgot to tell you that could happen."

"Why does your sister hate us?" she whines, blinking her eyes open.

95

"It's actually my fault," I say. "I volunteer at the shelter on Sundays, so Brighton's gonna give me a ride. She can drop you off on the way."

Normally, we all just walk home from our sleepovers, seeing as Luna, Zoey and I live five minutes away from each other. Things get a little more difficult with Jessa in the mix, because she lives on the other side of town. It's technically still walkable, because Middletown is tiny, but it's not the kind of walkable most parents would be cool with us doing alone.

Jessa's eyes open fully for the first time.

"Oh," she says. "I think my parents had plans this morning. I didn't think I'd be going back until later."

A lump forms in the pit of my stomach. How inconsiderate am I, to not even think about whether Jessa's parents would be cool with us dropping her off so early? Crap. Crap. Crap.

I force myself not to think too hard about what I say next.

"You could come to the shelter for a bit until you can get picked up?" I suggest. "Lydia wouldn't mind, but she'd probably put you to work."

It's not my greatest idea ever. I mean, first of all I wake Jessa up at the crack of dawn with no warning, and then I tell her if she doesn't want to inconvenience her family she has to pull a shift at the animal shelter? And *then* I'm going to take her *into the shelter*? Where Archie is? Where she could see right through my whole experiment?

I'm cringing even as I say it, but Jessa actually looks relieved.

"I'd love that," she says. "My mom'll make me shower for, like, an hour after because she's allergic to dogs, but she was going to do that anyway."

That explains why Jessa spent twenty minutes on the floor when she got here yesterday, rolling around with all of the pugs: she's suffering from dog deprivation. She only stopped after I warned her that Bonnie's bladder control isn't what it used to be.

"No offense, Noah, but next week we are absolutely not coming here." Luna yawns. "I need a full sleepover cycle to recover from these mornings."

On weekends we aren't at my house, I bike to the shelter if it's early enough in the year, or Brighton comes to give me a ride. I usually have to sneak out of Luna's and Zoey's rooms like a burglar.

"I'm gonna start honking the horn if you guys aren't down here soon," Brighton calls up the stairs. She's very protective of her sleep on the weekends. Usually after she drops me off, she comes right back home and sleeps some more.

"Do you remember when we put shaving cream on Brighton's pillow in the fourth grade?" Zoey asks. "I think we should do that again."

"Great idea," I say. "It almost got me murdered last time, so let's definitely try again when she's gotten bigger and stronger."

After two tired hugs with Luna and Zoey, Jessa and I climb into my family's minivan, where an extremely grumpy Brighton in extremely bright green pajama pants is waiting behind the wheel. Minnelli is sitting on the floor at her feet, breathing heavily. But she's an elderly pug, so she's always breathing heavily. Once I've buckled myself in, she slowly waddles over to my side and crawls into my lap.

Despite our slow start this morning, we make it to the shelter at my normal time. It isn't until Lydia lets us in that I start to get nervous.

"You know you're only supposed to bring *animals* to the shelter, right?" Lydia asks.

"Oh," Jessa says. "If you don't want me hanging around here, that's fine, I can call my parents—"

"I was just kidding!" Lydia says. Turns out, Archie's a great worker. Lydia now thinks any help I recommend is perfect, so I hope Jessa lives up to expectations. "You're all good. Noah, could you guys go help Archie clean up the rodent room?"

My heart picks up speed without my permission. I don't think Jessa's been as bad as Luna and Zoey with all the boy stuff recently, but I can't tell whether that's because I have less experience with how Jessa is normally. Maybe camp Jessa was a different, chilled-out version of herself, and now that she's settled into her new school she's going to morph into Boy Jessa just like Luna and Zoey did. I really, *really* don't want a shelter day to be taken over by my own anxiety that Jessa's reading into every interaction Archie and I have.

It's weird with Archie. It's not that I don't talk to guys in my class, but ever since we got to middle school it's been different. The guys got louder and more annoying, and it just felt like hard work to keep talking to them. Even Blake changed. Last year, he'd sit with us at lunch every day. Now, he's migrated over to a table with just boys.

But I don't know if Jessa would understand any of that. Or if she'd get why it feels weird to me, since it doesn't seem like it's weird to anyone else.

"Nice of you to show up," Archie says when we get into the rodent room.

"Did you make a set of keys?" I reply. "Lydia usually *barely* gets here before me."

"Guess I'm just not a slacker like you guys."

We both laugh, and Jessa, who'd been watching our conversation with a little furrow between her eyebrows, seems to realize that we're kidding around with each other and relaxes.

"My fault," she says. "Noah neglected to tell me that sleeping over at her house on Saturday nights comes with a wake-up call."

I haven't ever seen Jessa and Archie talk to each other in homeroom, but our school is small enough that they probably have other classes together. It's kind of weird to think about Jessa, who still seems so new and shiny and my own, making friends with everyone else at school. Sometimes it feels weird that she exists outside of my bubble.

"I assume that's after the hair braiding and boy gossip," Archie says. "Also, important to note that I have an aunt who used to babysit me a lot and so all of my knowledge of girl sleepovers comes from movies from the early 2000s."

"You've come startlingly close," Jessa deadpans, flashing Archie her new manicure courtesy of Luna.

"We even caught a glimpse of a *boy sleepover*," I say, rolling my eyes because I'm facing a couple of guinea pigs who would never narc on me. "So you can imagine how thrilled we are today."

"Oh god, was it that thing Blake had last night?" Archie asks. My ears perk up before I can help it.

"Blake had people over last night?" I ask. See, there it is again! Last year, if Blake was having a sleepover we'd all meet at the park near my house and hang out. Now I think we'd have to prepare for a month in advance to do the same thing.

"I didn't sleep over, but he invited me, which was . . . nice, I guess?" Archie shrugs. "I left after, like, an hour. It was pretty much just a group therapy session where everyone had to keep reassuring Blake that Luna likes him. I'm pretty sure I narrowly avoided him writing love songs."

"Ballads," Jessa suggests.

"Sonnets," I add with a laugh.

"Oh, I could have dealt with love songs *and* ballads," Archie says. "But I *draw the line* at sonnets."

Jessa and I break down into laughter, both of us covering our faces with our hands.

Huh. Hanging out with Archie and Jessa at the same time is much easier than I was worried it would be. If Luna or Zoey were here, I think I'd be overanalyzing every interaction with Archie to make sure she was *sure* I had a crush on him. Instead, Archie and Jessa hanging out so casually puts me at ease enough that it's probably my most convincing crush performance yet.

Jessa's phone chimes, and she pulls it out of her pocket and starts typing a message, smiling down at the screen.

I don't mean to be nosy, but before I can stop myself I ask, "Who're you texting?"

Yikes. I don't want Jessa to think that I'm, like, possessive over her or anything weird like that. I was just curious.

Jessa doesn't seem to think that I'm being weird. She finishes the message, hits Send, and then smiles up at me.

"Luna," she says. "She asked what I was doing so I told her we were all hanging out here."

At first, it feels really nice that Jessa's been enveloped into our little group so easily and made her own bonds with Luna and Zoey.

That nice feeling lasts about two seconds, though, because . . .

Oh no.

As if on cue, my phone dings. And then it dings again. And then it dings again. And again, and again, and again, and again.

I'm afraid to look, but I know letting the messages stack up will only make it worse.

Luna: You're WITH ARCHIE RIGHT NOW?????????

Zoey: OH MY GOD WHAT????????

Luna: JESSA JUST TOLD ME!!!!!

Zoey: Noah OH MY GOD you weren't going to tell us?????

Luna: She was probably too distracted to tell us

Luna: Distracted by LOVE

Zoey: STOP that's so cute WHAT ARE YOU GUYS TALKING ABOUT

It's too much. Later, when I'm home, I'll be able to muster the required levels of mysteriousness and I-definitely-have-a-crush-on-Archie-ness for this conversation, but I can't do it right now. Not at the shelter, the last place on earth where things still feel normal. I stuff my phone back in my pocket.

"I'm going to go see if Lydia needs help with the dogs, are you guys okay here?"

Jessa furrows her eyebrows like she's worried about me, but I try to ignore it. I'm fine. I know I'm fine. I just need to turn off my phone. And maybe not be around Archie *or* Jessa for a second, just to be safe.

I'm out the door before I can hear what they say in response, but no one follows me anyway.

12.

My Best Halloween Costumes, Ranked.

1. 2019: basket of laundry (I smelled like dryer sheets for a week straight)
2. 2017: lady who just got out of the shower (white balloons pinned to a bathrobe)
3. 2020: human garbage (trash bag with candy wrappers taped to it)

"Prince and princess?"

"Ew, that's so . . . typical."

"Princess and her unicorn?"

"Only if you're the princess."

"I could be a princess!"

I can hear Brighton and Marcus lightly bickering back and forth about their Halloween costumes before I even climb up the old attic ladder. I clipped a water bottle to the belt loops on my jeans, because the dust up here makes my throat itch, but I'm *ready* to spend my Saturday afternoon with my sister and her boyfriend.

Normally, I could probably take or leave a day like today. I love Brighton, and I like Marcus, but they have a tendency to be a bit . . . what's the word . . .

Incredibly annoying and lovey-dovey and disgusting.

However, today I've had to make an exception.

Now that Step Two has been enacted, it's only a matter of time before Step Four: Flirting. It's the step I've been dreading the most—I figure at least by the time we get to Step Seven (kissing), I'll like Archie enough to *want* to do it. Having to flirt with someone when you don't want to, *and* when you also have no idea how to flirt? I don't even know where to begin.

I'm no closer to having a crush on Archie *or* making him my boyfriend, which means the experiment has stalled out before we've even made it halfway through the method. So when Brighton said Marcus would be coming over this morning so they could figure out their Halloween costumes, I asked if I could hang out with them.

I know, logically, that flirting happens when you meet someone and decide that you want to date them, and then I guess you just flirt until the end of time. It's like in the wild, when animals grow colorful feathers or do intricate dances to attract a mate. I just need to figure out what the human version of that is. Brighton must have mastered it since she has Marcus, so now all I need to do is observe them.

Unfortunately, observing them means *observing them.*

By the time I make it up to the top of the ladder, Brighton and Marcus have stopped play-fighting with each other and Brighton's tucked up under Marcus's chin. The two of them are swaying gently back and forth.

Gross.

"Is this how it's going to be the whole afternoon?" I ask, crossing my arms. Brighton laughs into Marcus's chest before pulling away.

"Hey, Small Frye," Marcus says.

It wasn't funny the first time he said it, and it's not funny the millionth time, either. But Marcus is one of those annoyingly nice, cool people who can make you laugh at unfunny stuff like that, so even though I try to stop myself I smile at him in return.

"Are you guys seriously going out for Halloween dressed as a princess and a unicorn?" I ask.

"Yes," Marcus says.

"No," Brighton says. Marcus opens his mouth to argue, but Brighton laughs and says, "No, shut up! We are absolutely not doing that."

My family are Halloween People. I'm pretty sure everyone's family has a holiday that they inexplicably take seriously. Like, Luna's parents once accidentally cut power to the whole street when they turned on their Christmas lights. Our thing is Halloween. My parents start planning in the summer, and by the time school starts up my mom's usually hauling home armfuls of new supplies and fake cobwebs and fog machines. Actually, now that I think about it, that should have been my first sign that something was wrong with the business. We haven't bought a single new Halloween prop this year.

"So," Marcus says. "Remind me why we can't just go to a store and pick costumes from there?"

Brighton stills where she's squatting and trying to open an old, possibly haunted trunk that my dad brought home from an estate sale a few years ago.

"We're cooler than that," she says eventually. "Everyone's gonna have store-bought costumes. Let's make something better."

I snort. "Yeah, plus the fact that we can't afford—"

I cut myself off when Brighton jerks her head up to look at me. Her eyes are wide.

"Can't afford to keep killing the planet by buying these one-off polyester costumes," I finish. It's not the best save in the world, but I'm still pretty impressed with how quickly I came up with it.

"Noah's become very environmentally conscious lately," Brighton says.

"There's no plan B," I say.

"*Planet* B," Brighton corrects.

"Right."

So Brighton hasn't said anything to Marcus about the money thing. Interesting. I haven't told Luna or Zoey, but I thought you were supposed to share stuff like that with your partner. I give Brighton a look that lets her know she's not off the hook and I'll be asking her a ton of questions about this later. She rolls her eyes at me.

"That's why we're not buying any new decorations this year either," I add. I figure I might as well keep going if I'm on a roll.

"Great idea," Marcus says, smiling easily at me. He turns

around to look at Brighton and I shrug helplessly at her from behind his back.

"So now that we've cleared up the fact that our planet is dying," Brighton says, "can we get back to the costume plan?"

Sometimes Brighton likes to pretend like she's too cool for all the stuff our parents love, but it's too late for her. They've already created her in their image—she got all their best looks *and* their best personality traits, but that also means she's just as obsessed with Halloween as they are. I love it too, don't get me wrong, but I've never had that intense obsession that the rest of my family seem to have. I'm sort of just along for the ride.

It's only unfair if you think about it too hard, really.

Marcus opens his mouth to respond, but all that comes out is this weird, wheezy whine.

Wait, that can't be right.

I peek down the attic trapdoor to find Bonnie and Clyde standing at the bottom of the ladder.

"You guys can't come up here," I tell them.

Bonnie whines again.

"No, I mean you *physically* can't come up here," I repeat. "You can't climb ladders and you both have asthma. Go take a nap."

Bonnie and Clyde appear to think about it for a second. Then, they must remember that they're elderly pugs who can barely climb regular stairs, and that they *do* love naps, so they both trot off together.

"Which two were those ones?" Marcus asks, coming up

behind me and watching the two curly tails disappear down the hall. Marcus has been trying to figure out how to tell the pugs apart since before he and Brighton even started dating.

"Bonnie and Clyde," I tell him.

"Bonnie and Clyde!" Brighton exclaims from the depths of the attic.

Marcus and I whip around. Brighton has that look in her eye that means she has an idea.

"Bonnie and Clyde?" Marcus asks.

"Bonnie and Clyde," Brighton agrees. "It's couple-y, but still interesting. Plus, my mom has a bunch of vintage dresses up here; I'm sure at least one of them will work. It's perfect."

"You do know that they died in a fiery shoot-out, right?" Marcus asks.

Brighton rolls her eyes. "*You* know that Bonnie Parker's role in their crimes was played up for shock value in the press because she was a woman even though there's little evidence that she ever even fired a gun, *right*?"

Oh no. They might be at this for a while.

"I didn't know that," Marcus says, trying and failing to keep an extremely mushy smile off his face. "But we can't all be geniuses."

"*Clearly* not," Brighton replies, with a gooey smile. I avert my eyes as Marcus playfully yanks her closer and they kiss.

"Glad that's settled," I say, waving my hand around. "But what am *I* supposed to wear?"

I hate feeling like the annoying little sister. I'm perfectly capable of sitting in my room alone or going to a friend's house when our parents aren't home—Brighton hasn't been my babysitter in ages. Now that I'm old enough that we can just hang out as equals, I don't want to feel like I'm just tagging along.

"Well, that depends," Marcus says. "Will you *also* be needing a couple's costume?"

I groan louder than I mean to, throwing my head back and letting it all out because there aren't many places I can answer that question with this response anymore.

"So that's a no," Marcus says. Sometimes, he looks at me and he seems a bit freaked out. Like since I'll be thirteen next year and I'm a girl I'm liable to explode at any moment, and he just needs to make sure he isn't in the room when it happens.

"Noah doesn't need a boyfriend," Brighton says. She detaches herself from Marcus's side and walks over to wrap an arm around my shoulders. "Boys are gross, anyway."

"Can't argue with that," Marcus says.

I groan again (slightly more restrained this time), squirming out from under Brighton's arm.

"You guys don't have to do that," I say.

"Do what?" Brighton asks.

I roll my eyes. "That acting-like-I'm-a-little-kid, joking-in-front-of-me thing. You obviously don't think boys are actually gross, and that's *fine*. You're just making me feel weirder by pretending."

Brighton and Marcus exchange a look, and I consider

telling them about Archie to try to at least get some practice in. Except, I'm a bit exhausted and I figure if I have to start talking about him even *more* with Luna and Zoey, I might as well have a spot at home to *not* talk about him.

"Well, forget about boys, then," Brighton says. "Let's find you a Halloween costume so good everyone's going to understand that you're too cool for them anyway."

13.

Best Flirting Methods*

1. Bickering
2. Light insults
3. Physical contact
(*These methods have not been scientifically proven)

I spent most of Saturday observing how Marcus and Brighton flirt with each other, but I'm still not 100 percent sure I know what I'm doing. I get more and more nervous the closer I get to the shelter. By the time I'm locking up my bike outside, I've spiraled my way into a full-on anxiety swirl. I mean, how am I supposed to know if high school flirting and middle school flirting are different? Maybe if I modeled my sister's advanced technique, I'd end up embarrassing myself. Maybe it would make more sense to spend a couple of days studying up on how Luna and Zoey flirt, and ensure my method is in line with middle school standards, but now that it's October, Halloween is worryingly close. If Archie and I aren't kissing by then, all of this is going to have been for nothing, because the party is going to make it *very* clear that I'm not on the same level as everyone else.

At least I'm the first person at the shelter this morning.

Things are like how they used to be on shelter mornings; just me, Lydia, and a dozen litter boxes. I guess not all change is big and scary, because while I'm scrubbing the bottoms of cat toilets, all I can think is *I hope Jessa gets here soon.*

It didn't take Jessa long to fall in love with the shelter, the way I'd hoped Luna and Zoey would when they tried volunteering with me. Thankfully, Archie's been so helpful that Lydia didn't hesitate for a second when I asked whether Jessa could join the team too.

She's fitting in way better than I thought she was going to. It's not that Jessa isn't cool—she's the coolest—but she's cool in that grown-up way that can come off as standoffish sometimes. I spent the whole first week of camp worried that I was bothering her, never suggesting we do anything myself and waiting for her to lead the way. It wasn't until one night I made her laugh so hard that contraband whipped cream shot out of her nose that the illusion was shattered.

I know I should want to talk to her about everything. About how she's doing after moving so far away from her old school, about how she feels about being rolled in with my friend group, about how that friend group feels slipperier and slipperier by the day. It all just feels embarrassing, though. Feelings like that have always been weird for me. I'm happy to tell my friends I love them, but anything more or deeper than that starts to make me uneasy. I'm so worried, all the time, about someone thinking I'm weird or embarrassing. Sometimes it means I overcorrect. Nothing can be weird or embarrassing about me if you don't know much about me, right?

I don't *like* being this way, but here we are.

So when Jessa gets to the shelter and says, "Can I talk to you?" at first I think she's figured something out. I feel myself start to shrink, already getting ready to deny anything she guesses.

Except then I actually look at Jessa's face.

She looks just as uncomfortable as I do, grimacing and shifting her weight from foot to foot. I've never, *ever* seen Jessa look uncomfortable.

"What's wrong?" I ask, immediately ready to fist fight whoever made her feel like that.

Jessa seems to think about it for a while, weighing up her options. Eventually, though, she lets out a big breath and says, "Why are you being weird with me?"

Huh. I guess I have to fist fight myself.

"Weird how?" I say instead of anything resembling the truth.

Jessa sighs, exasperated. "It feels like ever since we got back from camp, you've gotten further and further away. At first I thought I was reading too much into things, but I don't think I am. We don't talk like we did at camp. It's almost like you're hiding something, but I have no idea what you'd be hiding."

I gulp.

There are two options here. First, I could tell Jessa everything and ruin the integrity of the experiment. It would get everything off my chest, but it would also probably make Jessa run screaming away from me.

Second, I could decide to *really* commit to the experiment.

And that's the option that *doesn't* end with Jessa running screaming away from me.

I know which one I like more, and it's the one that keeps Jessa around.

"I've just been feeling a little . . . nervous, lately," I say. "I see Archie every weekend and I have no idea whether he likes me back or not."

"And that's meant you can't talk to me anymore?" Jessa asks.

I ball my hands into fists, frustrated. Why does nothing come out the right way when I'm trying to talk to Jessa?

"I've never done the whole, like . . . crush thing before," I say. "I don't really know how to do it. It's kind of embarrassing. I don't want to annoy you with all of it."

Jessa bites her lip, looking at a spot on the wall behind me for a long moment. It's probably only a few seconds, but they all feel like they last at least an hour while I wait for her to reply. Finally, *finally*, she gives me a tiny smile.

"You don't annoy me," she says. "Ever. Just talk to me, okay? What's going on?"

Oh man. That means bringing out the big guns.

I hate the big guns.

"I really like Archie," I say. I try to sound as serious and in love as possible. "Like, a lot. I'm trying to start flirting with him more so he gets the picture, but I think I need, like . . . a wingman? Maybe you could help today?"

We look at each other for a long, long time. Jessa's eyes are so big when we're this close together. I realize I've stepped into her space again and take an awkward step back, which seems to snap Jessa out of it.

"You *really* like him?" she asks. "For real?"

I gulp, but try not to make it noticeable. Stretching the truth is one thing, but this would be really, actually lying to Jessa.

But aren't I at least a little justified here? If one lie could eventually turn into the truth?

"I really like him," I repeat.

Jessa takes a deep breath. She rubs at one of her eyes. And then she says, "Then I've got your back."

It's one thing to lie about the experiment to Jessa, but it's entirely another to maintain anything close to confidence when we both hear the door chime and we know Archie's gotten here. Jessa shimmies her shoulders at me and mouths *show time*. I stick my tongue out at her and try to gain back whatever it was I was just pretending to have.

Okay, I can do this. I have to keep telling myself that, soon, I'll *want* to do this. So what's the issue with getting a bit of practice in, right?

"Morning," he says. "Man, does it ever get easier to wake up this early?"

"How early did you really wake up?" I ask. "I mean, you're here *way* later than we are."

Archie's eyebrows wrinkle slightly, his shoulders deflating. I see Jessa grimace from the corner of my eye.

"I mean, I'm still here an hour before the shelter even

opens," Archie says. "Lydia said we don't even have a set time we have to be here by."

I don't say anything, because it's possible that I brought too much energy to my first attempt at flirting. Archie looks genuinely upset, which is definitely not something I observed happening with Marcus and Brighton.

"I don't think it matters," Jessa pipes in. "As long as we help out as much as we can while we're here."

"Yeah, that's what I was thinking," Archie says. He's still looking at me funny, and I avert my eyes.

Okay, so attempt number one wasn't my best work.

"Oh," Archie says after a long, extremely awkward pause. "Noah, look at this picture of Hank I took last night."

Oh no. This is going to be the greatest test of my flirting skills. How am I supposed to play it cool when *Hank* is involved?

Archie holds his phone out so I can see the photo on the screen. It's Hank curled up on Archie's couch. Archie's clearly been messing with him, because he has a knit blanket draped over him and wrapped around his head like a little scarf.

I bite the inside of my cheek to keep from squealing out loud. This is even harder than I thought it'd be. I try to take a deep breath without it being too obvious before I respond.

"He looks sad," I say. "Like *help me, my owner won't stop making me watch stupid web shows.*"

I laugh after I say it to try to soften it, the way Brighton does with Marcus. This time, Archie doesn't look upset, but he *does* seem a bit angry.

116

"All right," he says flatly. He puts his phone back in his pocket.

"No, I'm just joking!" I say. I can't help myself, but I try to stay on track all the same. "Just, like, poor Hank, sitting there when you press Play on the same Scandinavian YouTube video *again*, right?"

"Yeah, I get it," Archie says.

Archie doesn't say much else to me for the rest of our volunteer shift, but I figure I've at least planted the flirting seed, so I leave it be for now.

"I think we have to go and mop now," I say. "The dog room usually gets pretty nasty."

Instead of responding to me, Archie just walks out of the room. Jessa and I sit there in silence for a moment.

"Did that . . . go the way you wanted it to?" Jessa asks into the quiet.

I cringe. "I mean, it wasn't *ideal*. But I don't think it was awful, either."

Jessa gives me a dubious look. "You're the most confident person I've ever met," she says. "And I don't know if that's a compliment or not yet."

I don't feel like the most confident person anyone's ever met right now.

"If I was confident, I probably wouldn't have needed you to supervise my flirting attempts in the first place," I say. I try to laugh at myself a bit to distract from the fact that my cheeks are going pink.

"Yes, but even in the face of *total disaster*—and I want to clarify, again, that that's what that was—you're still ready to keep trying."

I can't even help it. I throw my head back and laugh, grabbing Jessa by the arm to steady myself.

"It was more flirting than we've done before," I reason. "Even if it *was* a total disaster."

"So you admit it was a disaster," Jessa says.

I snort again. "Shut up."

14.

Worst Flirting Methods*

1. Bickering
2. Light insults
3. Physical contact
(*This has **absolutely** been scientifically proven)

As Jessa and I are leaving the shelter, Lydia looks up at me from her front-desk chair.

"Noah," she says in a quiet, strange voice. "Can you come talk to me before you go?"

Jessa and I share a quick look. She was going to come over for a little while after our shift so that we could talk about Step Four (I might not be making much headway with Luna and Zoey as far as the experiment goes, but it's certainly upping my conversations with Jessa).

"I'll wait outside," Jessa says.

Lydia nods. "It won't take very long," she says. "Thanks for everything today, Jessa."

Once Jessa leaves, something about the energy in the room changes. Lydia sits up straighter. She has a weird look on her face that I can't quite place.

"Come sit," she says.

I sit on my chair across from her a little uneasily. I feel like I should be wearing a nicer outfit or something.

"How are you finding things with Jessa and Archie volunteering with you?" she asks.

My eyebrows furrow. Is that all she wants to talk to me about? Why does this feel like a police interrogation?

"Fine, I think." I know it's actually going really well, but something about having Lydia ask, *How are you finding things?* in that tone of voice makes me wonder if it's actually going horribly and I haven't realized it yet.

"I know it can be hard to share something that feels really special and like your own thing," Lydia says. "And you know I appreciate how much you've helped this place over the last few years . . ."

". . . but?" I ask. There's a definite *but* in that sentence.

Lydia sighs, looking up at the ceiling to collect herself for a second.

"Do you remember how you've asked me how old you have to be to become a paid employee here?"

I perk up. "Yeah, you said not until I was fourteen. Why, is that different now?"

Another sigh. "Look. I think you're great. You do really good work here. But I'll only hire people who work just as well with people as they do with animals, which means I *definitely* can't have someone who's bullying another volunteer on my staff."

I blink. "Wait, what?"

120

I don't mean to respond so casually, but what Lydia just said to me makes absolutely zero sense. *Wait, what?* is pretty much the best I can do.

"Archie went home early today," Lydia says. "He was pretty upset, so we talked it out for a long time. He didn't want to tell me about this, but he eventually admitted that the reason he was upset was because you weren't treating him fairly today. Is that fair to say?"

Oh my god.

My stomach drops all the way down to my feet when I realize what's going on.

I'm so bad at flirting that Archie thinks I hate him.

My face goes redder than it ever has in my life. I think if you held a marshmallow up to my cheek right now, you could make s'mores.

"I really don't want to lose you as a volunteer," Lydia says. "But if this is how you behave around your peers, that's not an attitude I want to have around."

I think I might actually throw up. I'm never in trouble, but I'm *especially* never in trouble with Lydia. And even if I *was*, it would never be because of *bullying*.

"Can I talk to Archie?" I ask. I'm about half a second away from crying, but I can spend that half second explaining to Archie what happened (well, not *explaining* explaining). "I know why he's upset, and I think it might be a misunderstanding. Before you kick me off the team, can I at least talk to him?"

Lydia purses her lips. "I was going to give you guys a chance to figure it out, but I'm putting Archie first here, okay? Archie has to be the one to tell me if he's comfortable working with you again. And if I hear about any other incidents going forward, you won't have another chance. Got it?"

"Got it," I say, fighting back tears. I don't want Lydia to think I'm trying to make myself cry for sympathy points or anything, so I scurry out the door before she can see me.

So, Jessa thinks this is hilarious.

We're biking back to my house after the most humiliating moment of my life with Lydia. Or, I should say, *I'm* biking back to my house, while Jessa stands on the back of my bike and leans forward to laugh directly into my ear.

"Oh my *god*," she says.

She sniffles—she's *actually* crying. There are *actual* tears in her eyes.

"I'm glad you find this funny," I say grouchily, turning down Main Street and willing a tidal wave to come out of the lake and swallow me whole.

Jessa hops off the back of the bike with no warning. I swear in surprise, sticking my legs out to catch myself before we both go down. We weren't moving that quickly, but *still*. Bike safety is a thing, Jessa.

Jessa comes around to the front of the bike, putting both of her hands on my shoulders and leaning in so that the fronts of our helmets are touching. She's so close that my eyes almost cross.

"Noah," she says, extremely seriously, "I need you to know that I don't just find this *funny*. I find it to be truly, genuinely, *the funniest thing I've ever heard in my entire life.*"

"Oh my god, shut up," I say, but I can't help but laugh, too. "Now I have to convince Archie that I'm not some kind of weirdo who just woke up one morning and decided I hate him."

By the time we get to my house, Jessa's just barely recovered from her laughing fit. Honestly, if I were her I'd probably be doing the same thing. Even I can see that this is actually pretty funny. But if I'm supposed to be the brokenhearted girl who doesn't know how to flirt, I should probably step it up a bit.

"Are you coming inside, or would you prefer to roll around outside in the grass laughing at me like a cartoon character?" I ask. I try to look a little hurt and add, "I really thought he was going to like me back, and now he thinks I hate him."

Jessa stops laughing right away, so at least there's that. She swallows hard and says, "Sorry. I didn't realize it meant that much to you."

I shrug. "I mean, it's not a *great* feeling."

She looks at me, assessing. I must look pathetic enough, because she nods to herself and says, "Then we aren't going inside."

"We're not?" I ask.

"Uh, no. We're going to Archie's house so you can apologize to him."

Obviously I was planning on apologizing to Archie, but I thought I could maybe do it via text. A call, if I must. I just don't know how I'm supposed to apologize for something that I can't explain. It's not like I can say, *Sorry, I was trying to flirt with you and it all went wrong. What's that? Do I like you? Not like that, no! Why do you ask?*

"Don't make that face," Jessa says. "We're going. If you want any chance of turning this around after that train wreck, you have to apologize in person, right now."

She hops back onto my bike, and I make my way to Archie's house. I spend the entire ten-minute bike ride running through possible apology scenarios in my head. None of them seem to end in my favor.

Hank barks when I ring the doorbell, and I briefly forget why I'm here because *oh my god, I get to see Hank.*

But then I see Archie through a window beside his front door, and when he realizes its me, he panics and tries to hide behind a corner in his house.

"Can I talk to you?" I cup my hands against the window so he can hear me. I'm half expecting his parents to come and kick me off their property, but instead Archie just peeks at me uneasily before going back to his hiding spot.

"Please?" I add. I try to make myself look as nonthreatening as humanly possible, but I think it's more like that time in elementary school when Zoey made me do the musical with her and I played an old lady who had to walk around all hunched over.

"Archie," Jessa shouts, coming up beside me. "She has a good reason, I promise."

For whatever reason, Archie seems to believe Jessa over me (the reason is most likely that Jessa was not the person who was just actively bullying him). He reluctantly comes to the door and opens it, but he doesn't invite me in. That's fair.

"I'm going to circle the block," Jessa says. "Please have resolved this by the time I return."

She hops down off Archie's porch and slowly bikes away.

"Technically she just stole my bike," I say. Archie doesn't reply, and I shake myself out of thinking about Jessa and into the task at hand.

"I'm so sorry," I say. "Really, really, really. What happened earlier was weird and messed up and I didn't mean to be mean to you or hurt your feelings."

"You didn't *mean to*?" Archie asks. "So, what, you did that accidentally?"

Well, yeah, kind of. In my head, this morning could've gone better, but it didn't seem like a complete wash. In my head, today Archie would be practically in love with me already.

I'm kind of stuck. Archie's looking at me expectantly, waiting for me to come up with the perfect answer that allows him to forgive me immediately. But I don't actually know the answer. Obviously I don't want to get fired from the shelter, but it's more than that. I genuinely value Archie as a friend now. I actually like him as a person.

Aw man, I can't lie to Archie. At least not fully.

"I was in a really bad mood," I say. "I shouldn't have taken it out on you, but I promise I won't do it again."

I wasn't really in a bad mood, but also, I've kind of been in a bad mood ever since I got home from camp and all of my friendships seemed like they were with totally different people.

Archie stares at me for a really long time.

"Why were you in a bad mood?" he finally asks.

I don't actually want to tell him this, but it's the only thing I can think of to say. Besides, maybe actually being honest with Archie for once could help with the plan. Or at least partially honest.

"My parents co-own a design and construction business," I say. "And with all the *Rural Refresh* crap going on in town, fewer people want to hire them. I guess we aren't doing so hot, money-wise."

I'm neon red saying that, but it's definitely better than telling Archie the full truth.

Archie's face falls slightly, but he doesn't look like he quite gets it yet. It's like he can't help being a good friend even when he wants to be mad at me.

"Luna and Zoey are putting a lot of pressure on my family's Halloween party to be some kind of Big Event," I say. "And I just felt overwhelmed, because I don't want to tell them the truth about it yet, but I'm also worried that they're going to leave me behind because our lives are . . . different."

There. Nothing I just said was technically a lie, but I didn't have to tell Archie anything that's going to make me want to skip town and change my name.

"I'm sorry," Archie says. "That must feel really awful."

He looks so sad for me, even though I was just so terrible to him. It almost makes me want to laugh. At least I picked a nice guy to be my future crush-slash-boyfriend.

"So are you still okay with working with me at the shelter?" I ask.

"Only if you promise to never react poorly to a picture of Hank ever again."

"Deal," I laugh.

Before I can thank Archie for talking to me and be on my merry way, something happens.

Archie steps forward and hugs me.

It's not like time stops and I finally realize my undying love for Archie as all the woodland creatures gather round to serenade us. It's kinda like when Luna or Zoey hugs me—it feels nice that my friend cares about me.

The hug barely lasts a second, just a quick squeeze, and Archie smiles at me before heading back inside. But *I* know that he just changed something, even if *he* doesn't know it.

All I have to do is tell Luna and Zoey about that hug, and it'll open up a whole new level of the experiment. Step Four will have been completed without my even needing to flirt (or try to flirt) in front of people who aren't Jessa.

Even though this wasn't my *exact* strategy, I've got to admit that it ended up working better than I thought. I mean, sure, I almost got in actual trouble and Archie was about to never speak to me again, but *after* that, I got a hug out of it. Which means he isn't disgusted at the thought of hugging me. When you think about it, this whole thing has actually brought us closer.

So take that, *Jessa*. And also, give me back my bike.

15.

Things You Aren't Allowed to Say to Theater People (or at least Zoey)

1. Good luck
2. You'll do great!
3. You've got this in the bag!

On Monday, I wake up to a text from Zoey in our group chat.

Musical auditions are today. If you aren't there you're dead to me.

"Drama queen," I say fondly down at my phone. Last year, we didn't go to her audition and Zoey didn't get a lead. Now she's convinced we're her good luck charms and we *always* have to be there.

"I wasn't expecting this from her," Jessa says to me at lunch, where both of us are sitting on either side of Zoey and rubbing her back while she's face planted on the lunch table. "She's normally so composed."

"I am extremely composed," Zoey says.

"You're seeing the behind-the-scenes view," I tell her. "To get the composed girl you'll see on the stage in a few hours, we first have to go through . . . whatever this is."

"Don't say *on the stage*," Zoey says. "It's bad luck."

129

"I don't think that's true," Jessa says. "I think it's bad luck to wish you good luck."

Zoey's head whips up to glare at Jessa in the same moment that she realizes her mistake.

"Take it back," she growls.

"I take it back," she says immediately. "Only bad luck. Bad luck, bad luck, bad luck."

The feeling in my chest only grows through the rest of the day. By the time Zoey's audition rolls around after school, my knee is bouncing and I don't know how to stop it.

Ms. Torentino, the drama teacher Zoey's obsessed with, moves to the front and claps her hands. She leans into the microphone to go over how the auditions work. Zoey's already standing to the side, squeezing her eyes shut and shaking her whole body. It's part of her warm-up routine, I know, but she looks like she's being abducted by aliens.

"If you're here to observe, I expect the utmost politeness," Ms. Torentino says. "Our performers deserve your attention. Now, please take a seat and keep your lips sealed."

I look around the gym and see Jessa sitting in a row of chairs set up in front of the stage.

"I thought you ditched me for a second," I whisper, plopping down beside her just as the lights go out except for the spotlight on the stage.

"Never," Jessa whispers.

Jessa and I sit through the first audition (pretty good, but nothing compared to what Zoey is capable of) in silence. I know that's what we're supposed to be doing, but the quiet isn't helping the anxiety coursing through me. It just gives me more time to stress. Like, should I have invited Archie to this? Would he have sat with us? Would he have held my hand in the dark? Would I have wanted him to? Would this have finally been the moment I figured it all out, and now I've missed my chance? Do you even get more than one of those moments with someone? Was it supposed to be *this* moment?

"Hey," Jessa whispers. Ms. Torentino is giving feedback to the girl who just sang, so there's basically no chance she hears her.

Jessa puts her hand on my knee, the one that I didn't realize was shaking.

Everything goes still. The only sounds in the world are my heartbeat and breath.

"What's going on?" Jessa asks, still whispering. The next girl gets on stage, and we both glance up to see if it's Zoey. It's not, so I take a breath and whisper my answer back to Jessa.

"I'm just . . . I don't feel well," I say. "Stuff with Archie is stressing me out. I can't tell if he likes me and I don't know what to do."

That's true, but not really for the reason I'm making Jessa think that it's true.

Jessa lets out a long, slow breath. She doesn't say anything for so long that I start to worry I've said something to annoy her, or even hurt her feelings somehow. But when I look over at her face, she's staring straight ahead, looking at the girl singing onstage but not really watching her.

"Just sit here," she finally whispers. I have to strain to hear her, her voice just barely rasping out. "Just . . . sit here for a second and don't think about Archie."

That's easier said than done. Hearing Archie's name makes me think about how much I *want* to like him, and thinking about that makes me think about how frustrated I am at the fact that I don't.

"Noah," Jessa mutters. She must have been able to tell that I definitely wasn't just sitting here not thinking about Archie. "Think about anything else. Or nothing at all. Just sit here with me."

I know that she's right, and that I should at least *try* to do what she's suggesting. I try to get comfortable in the hard plastic chair. It's not so easy, so I slouch down slightly and rest my head on Jessa's shoulder.

She startles a little, but Jessa always jumps just a tiny bit when I lean on her or hug her or grab her by the arm. I've known her long enough now that I know she'll tell me if she doesn't want me touching her.

She doesn't tell me anything like that. She seems to relax, leaning further into me. Being this close, I can smell that she uses vanilla shampoo and hear her nose whistling faintly each time she breathes in.

I listen to the rise and fall of Jessa's breath long enough that mine starts to match and before I know it I'm a million times calmer than I was a minute ago. I could fall asleep like this, actually. It reminds me of that awful night when my parents first told me about the problems with the business, the way Jessa helped me calm down and how I wished she was there with me to tell me things were going to be okay in person.

I must actually doze off, because a little while later I hear *Noah* in Jessa's raspy whisper and my eyes flutter open. I blink against the bright stage spotlight and realize that Zoey's up next.

"Get ready," I whisper to Jessa. "She's incredible."

Zoey opens her mouth to sing, and I can't help but reach out again and put my hand on top of Jessa's on my knee.

16.

What Makes Canadian Thanksgiving Different from American Thanksgiving

1. It happens in October
2. We have no idea why we celebrate it
3. We also have no idea why it happens in October

On the Saturday morning of the Thanksgiving long weekend, I wake up to the smell of roasting vegetables and pumpkin pie, and also to the sound of Brighton losing her mind.

"You didn't even buy a turkey?" she's yelling from downstairs. "So, what, he'll just have to eat all of our weird *sides*?"

I don't hear my dad's response, but I assume it must have been something along the lines of *we have a Tofurkey*, because Brighton just screams, "*TOFURKEY?*"

Right. Marcus is coming over for Thanksgiving dinner.

It's the first time he'll be directly involved with a Frye family holiday, which means I've already been told no fewer than seven times that if I want to eat dinner, I have to look presentable.

That's the exact quote. *Look presentable.* I don't think Brighton understands that her definition of *presentable* is very different from mine.

Y'know what? It's the first day of a long weekend. Thanksgiving dinner isn't until the early afternoon. I've got some time.

I change out of my normal pajamas and try to put together the weirdest outfit I can imagine. I pair purple leggings with my orange sweat shorts and top the whole ensemble off with my tie-dyed camp shirt that Brighton hates.

I walk downstairs, trying to act as nonchalant as possible, and sit at our dining table without looking at Brighton.

My dad figures out what I'm doing right away.

"Morning, sunshine," he says. "You look great today."

I beam. "Thank you!"

Brighton looks at me, and then my dad.

"I don't have time for this today," she says. "That's not what you're wearing."

"Oh, I think it is," I say. I look at our dad. "Right, Dad?"

He shrugs. "Who am I to hinder your self-expression? If this outfit is the physical representation of how Noah feels today, then I think that's beautiful."

"Thank you, Father," I say again, trying to look as angelic as possible.

Brighton scowls, looking back and forth between us.

"I hate you both," she determines.

"Well, then my work here is done!" I chirp.

My dad passes me a banana on my way back upstairs (he doesn't have many rules, but we always, *always* have to eat breakfast), and I eat it while rummaging through my drawers for my real outfit. As much fun as it is to mess with Brighton, I'm not *actually* going to try to ruin her first boyfriend Thanksgiving.

I video call Jessa when I can't think of anything to wear, and she picks up right away.

"Happy Thanksgiving weekend!" I say.

She doesn't respond, and I can hear a bunch of adult voices talking over each other. She mouths *one sec* into the camera and then stuffs her phone into her pocket, if the way the screen goes dark is any indication. When she returns, she's in her bedroom (I think. I still haven't seen her house, but I can see her gray headboard and the same white walls from the last time we video chatted).

"Sorry," she says. "My parents had, like, everyone they've ever met over last night and everyone's still here."

"I miss you," I blurt out. I don't mean to say it, but this is technically the longest amount of time I've gone without seeing Jessa since school started. I'm used to having long weekends away from Luna and Zoey, but it's different with Jessa.

"Sorry," I say. "Was that kind of ridiculous? I know I saw you yesterday. But my sister's losing her few remaining marbles and I wish you were coming over today instead of Marcus."

Jessa's whole face softens. She tucks part of her hair behind one ear and says, "Yeah, I wish that too, actually."

We kind of just smile at each other for a little while, but Jessa breaks first.

"I mean, it *is* kind of ridiculous. But I don't care. I guess I'm ridiculous too."

That's what I love about Jessa. She never makes me feel weird or like I'm too much. Like, back in third grade, we had a new girl join our class named Kendal, and I thought she was really cool and I wanted to be her friend *really badly*, and we hung out a few times but then after a while she started acting weird around me. She made me feel like I was obsessed with her or something. Like I was annoying her just because I wanted to be her friend. She moved away after we finished fourth grade, and I was happy that she wouldn't be around anymore because I started to feel weirdly embarrassed whenever I saw her, like I was the problem there even though I'm pretty sure I wasn't.

"What's Brighton doing?" Jessa asks.

I roll my eyes. "She wants Thanksgiving dinner to be this extra special event to make it perfect for Marcus. She just got mad at our dad for serving tofurkey. Like, every single person in this family is a vegetarian. Did she think my dad was going to go out and butcher a wild turkey just so that her boyfriend wouldn't have to ingest soy?"

Jessa laughs so hard she snorts. "Sorry," she says, covering her mouth self-consciously. "I've just never heard the word *tofurkey* said with such rage before."

I laugh with her. Another thing I love about Jessa: she always helps me find the humor in a situation.

"I just don't understand why it's so important," I say. "He has dinner with us at least twice a week."

"It's probably different though, right?" Jessa says. "Like, going over to someone's house is one thing, but this is a holiday. Your family probably takes pictures. It's all really official."

I pretend to gag and Jessa laughs.

"I think it's kind of nice," she says. "Don't you think? I think it would be cool to have someone you liked so much you wanted to include them in family stuff."

I groan. "Not you too! Don't tell me I have yet *another* reason I need to be official with Archie, like, yesterday."

Jessa blushes. "I'm not talking about anyone specifically," she says. "I just think *in theory* it would be nice to have someone that you like that much and who likes you back just as much. Y'know?"

I don't think I've ever really thought about it like that before.

"Yeah, I guess," I concede. "In theory."

Jessa chews on her bottom lip for a second. She only does that when she's thinking really hard about something.

"Do you think maybe you've ever—"

"NOAH!"

Brighton's yell and pounding on my door interrupts whatever Jessa was about to ask me. I roll my eyes at Jessa apologetically.

"Sorry," I say. "I have to go see what her highness wants."

Jessa swallows down whatever it is she was going to say, giving me a tiny smile.

"Keep me updated," she says.

I salute her and hang up.

Brighton's still banging on my door hard enough for my entire room to shake, but I'm used to her dramatics. I calmly walk to the door and swing it open. Bonnie and Clyde come running into my room and hide under my bed. They have an impressive sock collection under there and I've learned it's best to not intrude on their sanctuary.

"Oh, hey, Brighton," I say. "Have you been waiting long? So sorry, I couldn't hear you."

What Brighton said downstairs earlier was clearly true: she does *not* have time for me. Unfortunately for her, that's when I really shine.

"Marcus is going to be here in five minutes," she says. "I need you to show me what you're wearing today so that I can tell you whether it's normal."

"Rude."

"But not uncalled for," she counters, gesturing at the purple leggings I'm still wearing. "Exhibit A."

"I wasn't *actually* going to wear them," I say.

"No, but the fact that you own them at all is reason enough for me to worry."

"Why is he coming so early?" I ask. "We aren't eating for, like, four hours."

"Because when someone likes spending time with you, they want to spend *more* time with you."

I sit on my bed, crossing my arms in front of my chest.

"Why don't you just save us both the time and tell me what I *can* wear," I say.

Brighton nods, spinning around and going through my dresser until she finds a pair of burgundy pants that she thrifted for me last year, but I've never worn, and an old T-shirt from a musical festival I stole from my dad.

"Tuck the shirt in, but keep it baggy," Brighton instructs. "Roll up the sleeves."

Rats. That's really cute.

Thankfully, I don't need to admit to Brighton that she chose well, because as soon as I've grabbed the clothes from her the doorbell rings and all the color drains from Brighton's face.

"No one answer that!" she screeches. She sprints out of my room, slamming my door behind her, and thunders down the stairs.

I get changed quickly because there's no use in prolonging the inevitable.

Marcus looks up when I come down the stairs and gives me double finger guns. It's annoyingly charming.

"Hey, Small Frye," he says. "Cool shirt."

"Thank you," I, Brighton, and our dad say at the same time.

"Pretty sure he was talking to me," I say.

"I picked the shirt," Brighton says, shrugging.

"I believe *I* picked the shirt," Dad counters. "When you both were but a twinkle in my eye. When I was young and carefree and didn't have a teenager living in my home who told me what I could and could not wear to the Thanksgiving dinner *I* cooked."

"You must miss those days," I say, just to annoy Brighton. I figure she deserves a bit of extra annoying little-sister energy since she interrupted my conversation with Jessa.

My dad wraps his arm around my shoulders and squeezes me to his side, sighing with a far-off look in his eye. It's all very dramatic.

"I do," he says, and I laugh, squirming out from under his arm and wandering into the kitchen.

Our kitchen table has exploded, apparently. In its path of destruction, the only thing left is the biggest table arrangement

I've ever seen. You can barely tell that there's a table underneath all of the flowers and tiny pumpkins and place settings with, like, four plates of different sizes all stacked on top of each other. I didn't even know we *had* that many plates.

"She must be stopped," I mutter, and my mom laughs.

I jump a little; I didn't know that she was even in the kitchen. Cooking stresses her out and she normally lets my dad handle it, especially on holidays.

"She just wants to make a good impression on Marcus," my mom says.

"She did that already. They're dating."

"This kind of thing is different," she says. "A bit more serious."

She has an extremely annoying *you'll understand when you're older* tone to her voice, so I decide to immediately remove myself from this conversation. Liza and Minnelli are sniffing around at my feet, so I take them outside. It's not too cold yet, and if I wear a coat, I can kill some time sitting on our back deck and watching the geese migrate.

I go to the front door to grab my coat, but on my way I hear Brighton talking.

"They're so annoying," she's saying.

Okay, rude. I wasn't planning to eavesdrop on her conversation, but now I have to.

"They aren't annoying," Marcus says. *Thank* you. "You're just stressed out."

I peek just slightly around the corner to see Brighton

141

standing with her arms wrapped around Marcus's middle. Her face is squished into his chest and he's shifting his weight from foot to foot so that they're swaying a little together. Almost like they're dancing, or floating, or dreaming.

Brighton's laugh is muffled since her face is squished.

"I just wanted you to have a nice time," she says. "I don't want to look at pictures from this Thanksgiving and be like *oh, and there's Brighton's boyfriend that we all scared off.*"

"I'm already having a nice time. I always have a nice time."

"You don't have to eat the food if you don't like it. Seriously, don't worry. You aren't veggie. You should have a normal Thanksgiving dinner."

Marcus pulls away from Brighton and looks her in the eye. He puts a hand on either side of her face, scratching at the back of her head lightly.

"Bee," he says. "I truly, genuinely could not care any less about Thanksgiving. I'll eat whatever your dad puts in front of me. I'm just happy you like me enough to invite me in the first place."

Brighton laughs. "Don't be ridiculous, of course I like you that much."

Marcus doesn't answer that. Instead, he wraps Brighton up in another big hug, swaying them back and forth again.

I turn around and run outside without my coat on.

That was . . . different. That was weird. Or maybe I feel different? Or maybe nothing's weird except for me?

I think about what Jessa said to me earlier. *It would be nice to have someone you liked that much.* I had agreed because I didn't want Jessa to think that I didn't understand, but I didn't know what she was talking about, not really.

Seeing Brighton and Marcus just now—they were both so happy to just be standing beside each other.

I want someone to be that happy to be near me. I want to be that happy to be near someone and squish my face into them.

Whatever it was that I just saw, I want it.

17.

Possible Post-Thanksgiving Activities

1. Napping
2. A brisk walk in the great outdoors
3. Decorating for Halloween*
(*This is obviously the best one)

So, this epiphany complicates things slightly.

I had a brief panic over dinner that my realization meant that I was in love with Marcus. Like, maybe the thing I wanted wasn't the relationship, it was the guy I saw. I mean, the first time I even realized it would be nice to have a relationship like that was while I was spying on Marcus, so even though I've never *ever* thought about him that way, I still spent half the time sneaking glances at him and trying to decide whether I felt any differently. And then he choked on a spoonful of mashed potatoes, coughing it out onto my plate from across the table, and that ended that worry.

The actual difference is that now my experiment is even more important. Now I can see what I might be able to have if it works. I could barely focus after dinner because I was thinking about what it would be like if someone hugged me the way Marcus hugged Brighton. I've seen them PDA-ing all over the place before, but this felt different. I've never seen the calming effect he has on her firsthand like that. And she looked so happy to be around him.

What it would be like if someone touched my face like that? How would it feel if someone scratched at the back of my head when I was stressed out?

Now, you may be wondering: Did any of those thoughts involve Archie, specifically, doing those things? Not really. I imagined a sort of gray scribble in my head where the other person would go. But all things considered, Archie's my best shot at experiencing those feelings now that I actually want them.

Which means that now, there's even more at stake.

"Do we have enough food?"

I look up at my dad. I look down at our kitchen table—thankfully, long since cleared of Brighton's Thanksgiving decorations. Instead, our Thanksgiving leftovers, desserts, and any other frozen snacks my parents could dig up from the chest freezer in our basement cover every available molecule of the table's surface.

"I can't tell if you're joking," I say.

Thanksgiving is a big day in the Frye household. But not because of Thanksgiving.

We used to start decorating for Halloween way in advance (like, end of August "way in advance"). But then a few old ladies down the road started to complain, and my mom got too into it one year and someone thought the old witch we put in the tree in the front yard was real and called the cops, so we had to adjust our timeline. Now, we decorate as soon as we've finished Thanksgiving dinner, and Brighton and I are instructed to invite as many friends as we want over. It's usually a mixed crowd, depending on who's in town for Thanksgiving and who has their dinner on Sunday versus Saturday, but it's still fun.

My parents like to pretend that part makes them cool, fun parents, but it didn't take very long for our friends to realize that my parents only wanted their free labor.

Brighton and Marcus are in charge of carting down the dozens of decor boxes we have up in the attic with our mom, and I've been put on snack duty with my dad (you almost fall through the attic trapdoor *one time* and then suddenly no one trusts you with anything). The front door is open so that guests can come and go as they please. It's a nice gesture, but it mostly means that it's freezing in our house. I think if my dad had it his way, this is what life would always be like. He gets very excited when he's able to feed people and also decorate for Halloween.

"Hello?" Zoey's voice calls from the front of the house.

Zoey, Luna, and Blake are all standing in the doorway. Behind them, two cars are pulling into the driveway. I squint and make out Jessa and a blurry shape that's probably her mom in one, and a couple of Brighton's friends in another.

"I hope you're all hungry," I say in greeting. "And I'm not saying that because I'm trying to be a good host. I'm saying that because my dad will *absolutely* make me eat all the gross, soggy leftovers with him tomorrow so that nothing goes to waste."

"I'm on it," Blake says, charging ahead of us into the kitchen.

We all laugh, but Luna laughs the loudest.

"It's nice that he came," I say. I say it mostly because I know I'm supposed to. Blake was here last year, and the year before, and the year before that too, because he just comes to this stuff. He always has.

"He loves this," Luna says. She's still watching the hallway where Blake disappeared, as if he's going to come running back and sweep her up in his arms.

"He loves Noah's dad," Zoey laughs.

"It's true," I say. "You've got some competition for Blake's heart, Lunes."

"I should just give up now, then." Luna shrugs. "No one can compete with Mr. Frye's brownies."

Ooh, I forgot he made brownies today.

Jessa and Brighton's friends make it to the front door at the same time, just as my mom carries the last box of decorations downstairs.

"Perfect timing!" my mom says. "We're going to split into groups—divide and conquer. Noah, you and your friends are taking the front porch. Brighton, your group has the tree. Your father and I will do windows and yard."

Gee, I wonder where I get my tendency to execute a plan from.

Brighton gestures for her friends to turn around, and all three of them walk out to the front yard. One of them says something that makes everyone laugh, and when Marcus comes out to join them, he picks Brighton up around her middle and swings her back and forth. She slaps at his hands to try to get him to put her down, but everyone knows she doesn't actually want that.

"Noah?"

I'm startled out of my reverie by Jessa, who's standing in front of me and waving her hand in my face.

I shake my head. "Sorry!" I say, trying to sound as sunny and positive as possible. Luna, Zoey, Jessa, and I all sit on my front porch and await further instruction. It doesn't take long, because my mom's plans always run like well-oiled machines (I guess I didn't inherit *that* part) and she's in front of us practically before we even sit down.

"I'm giving you creative freedom with the porch," she says. "It can't be too scary, because this is where we'll be handing out candy. The last thing we need is a repeat of The Incident of 2015."

I have nothing but good memories from Halloween 2015, but my mom briefly has a far-off look in her eye, like she's reliving something horrifying.

"Mom?" I say.

"Sorry," she says. "Anyway, make it spooky, but not traumatizing. Deal?"

We all nod.

"Aren't we missing someone?" Mom asks.

"Blake's helping in his own way," I say. "And by that, I mean *Blake's currently eating every piece of food we have in our kitchen.*"

"Roger that," my mom says, and then turns around and

goes back in the house. Presumably to grab Blake and my dad from the kitchen and put them to work.

But she must make a pit stop, as once she's gone inside, our porch speaker starts playing "Monster Mash," and I know that's her favorite song.

"I found the fake spiderwebs," Luna says. "But they're gross, so someone else is gonna have to put them up."

"I think this bin is all those little witches that move when you walk by them," Zoey says, lifting up a bin's lid. She opens it a little more, and the sound of dozens of motion-activated Halloween decorations cackling at once fills the air. She screams and shuts the lid tightly again.

"What new stuff did you guys get this year?" Luna asks. She looks around like she'll suddenly see a new giant animatronic zombie somewhere.

I avert my eyes. Thankfully, I've already thought of my excuse for that question in advance.

"We ran out of space in our attic to store all of this stuff," I say. "So nothing new this year."

"Booooo," Zoey says. "I wanted *thrills!*"

I know she's joking, but it still stings. It's basically a confirmation that the party isn't going to be as cool as she and Luna are hoping it's going to be.

When Archie's mom pulls onto our street and I see Hank's big, perfect face hanging out of the window, I'm instantly more excited to see him than I am to see anyone else here.

"My baby!" I yell, running across the yard to give Hank a

million kisses on his beautiful nose.

"Yes, yes, I'm here," Archie says from the front seat. "You don't need to be *that* dramatic."

I laugh, but then I wonder if I shouldn't have laughed. Was Archie flirting just then? Should I have flirted back?

Ugh.

"Hey," Jessa says, coming up behind me with her arms crossed. "Luna wants to know how many pumpkins you guys are putting out this year. Something about the Great Pumpkin Pyramid Collapse of 2019? Why does everything have a *name* with you guys?"

"You weren't there!" Zoey screams from the front porch, pretending to be absolutely traumatized just because a couple dozen pumpkins came rolling down off my porch, nearly bowling over seven-year-old her.

Okay, so it wasn't *great*. But she was fine.

"I'll pick you up in a couple of hours," Archie's mom says, and Archie hops out of the car.

"Bye, Hank! I love you!" I call as the car pulls away, just to annoy Archie. He rolls his eyes at me, but he's grinning.

"All right," he says. "Put me to work."

"Don't let my mom hear you," I say. "You'll be here all night."

Was *that* flirting? God, I hope not. That would be weird.

The three of us head back up to the front porch, where Luna and Zoey are practically drowning in fake spiderwebs and obscured by fog emanating from my mom's machine. Blake's out here now too, balancing a plate stacked high with whatever he pillaged from the kitchen in one hand and a plate filled with cookies in the other. I realize he brought one out for Luna.

That's annoyingly cute.

"Newbies!" Blake calls out to Jessa and Archie. I mean, I think that's what he says. His mouth is full.

"Now you'll finally understand why Noah is the way she is," Luna says. I stick my tongue out at her, but she's right. That's part of why I invited Archie in the first place. I know that my family can be a bit much for some people—I love them, and I think we're all awesome, but not everyone would be this excited to decorate for Halloween immediately after Thanksgiving dinner. Not everyone takes my dad's random musings on life and nature in stride. Not everyone loves the fact that, no matter how well cared for they are, the pugs always have a certain . . . funk. And it's just that Marcus fits in with us so perfectly, accepting our quirks like he did at Thanksgiving and reminding Brighton how much he cares for her. If Archie can't handle Frye Family Halloween, I might as well call the whole plan off now.

"Honestly, she's not wrong," I admit, and Jessa and Archie laugh. "So, my mom said we can do whatever we want as long as it doesn't give little kids nightmares. Basically, we can start by going through the bins and then just . . . spookifying everything."

"Is that the technical term?" Archie asks.

"It is, thank you for asking."

Everyone busies themselves opening the bins and checking

out what's inside. It feels like every year I forget about all the stuff we have, and I'm starting to feel just a bit self-conscious about it. I know no one else here has this many Halloween decorations at home.

"Thanks for inviting me," Jessa says, nudging my hip with hers. We're the only two people standing, everyone else kneeling over their bins, so if my mom asks, I'll say we're supervising.

"Are you kidding me?" I scoff. "Of course I invited you. I always want you around."

I blurt it out without really thinking about it, but then I realize how true it is. I *do* always want Jessa around.

"I didn't know you invited Archie to this," she says, looking over to where he's accepting half a samosa from Blake. "Skipping right ahead to Step Six, huh?"

It kind of warms my heart that Jessa has the steps of the experiment's method memorized.

"Desperate times," I sigh. "I was pretty sure that by the time decorating night came around, Archie and I would basically be in love. I think I need to speed up the process a bit."

Jessa doesn't say anything, but she has a look on her face that almost seems upset.

"Sorry I didn't tell you," I say. "I figured you'd already done a lot for the experiment and I didn't want to bother you."

Jessa scrunches up her face. Now she looks kind of mad at me, which makes me panic because the *last* thing I ever want is for Jessa to be *mad at me*.

"Can I talk to you over here for a second?" she asks, gesturing down the path leading to the side of my house, where no one's paying attention to us.

"Sorry to be dramatic," she says. "I just figured you'd want to talk about this somewhere people couldn't overhear."

Jessa's so great. It's so nice to have a friend who—

"Ow!"

Okay, scratch that. Jessa just reached out and flicked me in the forehead.

"What was that for?" I demand, rubbing at the spot.

"Stop thinking that I'm going to be annoyed by you just because you talk to me about stuff!" Jessa says. "I'm your friend, aren't I? I haven't gotten annoyed at you yet, have I?"

I really, really didn't think she'd care, but she seems a little hurt by this.

"I'm sorry," I say.

Jessa doesn't respond right away, crossing her arms and looking away from me, over my shoulder at Brighton and her friends, who are busy wrapping lights around our oak tree.

"I just don't understand why you're so worried that I'll suddenly lose interest in you," Jessa says eventually. "What about me makes you think I'd do that?"

I feel my face start to heat up. I know I'm going to have to just tell the truth here, but the truth is kind of embarrassing.

"Luna and Zoey and I were kind of like . . . a given, y'know?" I ask. "When we were little kids, it was just easy to all be best friends because we all lived so nearby and we all liked hanging out with each other. I mean, when you're little that's pretty much all you need. I've never really had to . . . work for them. That's why it's been so weird lately. I've never had to put up this much effort just to try and be normal with them."

"And you don't want to work for me?" Jessa asks.

"No!" I say, wanting to do anything to wipe the hurt look off her face. "It's not like that. I just mean that Luna and Zoey and I are used to each other. They know that my family's weird and that I can get a bit obsessive over things and make a lot of intense plans and they've already decided to stick around. You could still decide to walk away."

Ugh, being vulnerable makes me itchy.

Thankfully, though, it's worth it. Jessa's face clears. She uncrosses her arms and she puts her hands on my shoulders.

"I'm here," she says. "I'm sticking around. I decided *ages* ago."

We smile at each other for a while, but then Jessa gets this glint in her eye.

"So *talk to me!*" she says, shaking my shoulders hard enough to move my entire torso. I shriek and try to pull away, but she moves her hands to my waist and tries to pick me up. She gets more lift than I think she will, but then we both topple to the ground.

The grass is wet and muddy and I'll definitely have to change my clothes after this, but I don't care. I turn to look at Jessa. The sun's setting, and I want to take a picture of her in this light, streaks of gold running across her face and lighting her blond hair up. She's looking back at me and I can't tell what she's thinking.

"All right," Jessa says. She sits up, even though that means the butt of her jeans is *absolutely* going to be completely covered in mud and dirt and fallen leaves. "Help me up so your mom doesn't yell at us for not decorating."

If I was given the choice between staying down there in the mud with Jessa and getting up to see everyone else, I know what I'd choose. But I help her up anyway, and we go rejoin everyone in the front yard.

18.

Reasons Your Sister Might Suddenly Start Being Nice to You

1. She's dying
2. You're dying
3. She wants something from you

I know something suspicious is afoot the second I wake up the next morning.

It may sound dramatic, but it's true. Sometimes you just wake up and immediately know that something's off, and today is one of those days.

First of all, I don't have my usual excited, blissed-out Sunday-morning feeling. Even though I'm going to the shelter today, Jessa won't be there. It'll just be me and Archie, but that means I'll have to try and make progress in the experiment, which sounds exhausting right now.

Second, I check the weather every night before I go to bed, and it was supposed to be sunny all day today. Instead, I hear rain pounding against my bedroom window.

Third, and most importantly, the reason I wake up is because Brighton is knocking on my door.

Brighton. Knocking. At six in the morning. On a *Sunday*.

My eyes narrow. I pull my duvet up to just under my eyes,

in case this is part of an elaborate prank and Brighton's going to come take pictures of me in my pajamas to post online or something.

"What?" I call. If Brighton *is* planning something, it's best to stay put so as not to walk into a trap.

"Train's leaving in ten minutes," Brighton calls back through the door.

Hm. It's not strange that she's giving me a ride, but it *is* strange that she doesn't seem grumpy about it.

"What about breakfast?" I ask. I still don't trust this.

"We'll stop and get something on the way," she says. "My treat."

Okay, now this is officially the weirdest interaction I've ever had with my sister. Who is this person who wakes up early to drive me places and offers to buy me food?

I don't trust it at all, but I also know that Brighton's my only chance to actually get to the shelter today (post-Thanksgiving, I pretty much have no hope of getting my parents to let me ride my bike in the cold), so I kind of have to go with it. Thankfully, ten minutes is plenty of time for me to brush my teeth, put my hair up in a bun, and slap on a pair of leggings and my shelter hoodie with VOLUNTEER written across the back. Showering can wait until after I get home, even though I know the thought would horrify Brighton. I disconnect my phone from its charger, stick it in my hoodie pocket, and traipse downstairs with five minutes to spare.

Brighton's sitting at the bottom of our staircase waiting for me, but she stands up when she hears the stairs creak.

"Ready to go?" she asks.

I look at her carefully. "Why are you being so nice to me?"

She sputters. "What do you mean? I'm always nice to you!"

"You're, like, sister-nice to me," I say. "Where it's *nice*, but you might decide to kill me at any moment. This is *nice* nice."

"You think I'm going to *kill you*?"

"The chances are low, but never zero. You have a lot of connections in this town and you know all my secrets, so you could definitely at least do some damage."

Brighton looks at me for a second like she has no idea what to do with me. There we go. That's more like the Brighton I know and love.

We rush outside through the rain to Mom's car and blast up the heat and radio at the same time. Brighton's shivering, even though we were only outside for two seconds.

"So!" she says once we're on the road. I don't like her tone. It reminds me of our parents when they're trying to get information out of me. "Yesterday was fun, right?"

I twist in my seat to look at her.

"Look, I appreciate the fact that you're giving me a ride, and that you're going to buy me breakfast. But you and I both know you want something from me, and the sooner you tell me what it is the sooner I can decline to answer."

Brighton looks at me dubiously.

"Have you been watching mafia movies?" she asks. "That was a very intense reaction to your sister buying you a bagel."

She pulls into the drive-through lane, but the line is a million cars long, which means I'm stuck with her.

"You can laugh at me all you want," I say. "But you're trying to get something from me."

"I'm not trying to get anything from you!" She laughs. "No offense, but what could I possibly want from you?"

I scrunch up my face. "That's not very nice. I have many gifts and talents."

". . . Okay."

The two of us sit in silence for a few moments, trapped in a stalemate. We move up one car length, then two, without saying a word to each other.

"I'm not trying to get anything from you," Brighton repeats when she finally speaks. "*But—*"

"*Ha!*" I say. "I knew there was a *but*."

"This really isn't as sinister as you're making it out to be," she says. "I just saw you hanging out with your friends yesterday and I wanted you to know that if there was ever anything you *wanted to tell me*, I wouldn't tell Mom and Dad. You know that, right?"

Oh.

Is Brighton saying what I think she's saying? Is my hypothesis actually starting come true?

(To everyone around me, at least.)

"You mean, like . . . if I had a crush on someone, or something like that?"

I wonder if it ever gets less embarrassing to say the phrase *crush on someone*. Maybe one day when I'm older, I'll be cool and totally fine talking about boys I like, but for now the whole thing just feels kind of gross and wearying for no reason.

Brighton smiles. It almost looks like she's going to cry and I really hope she doesn't. I don't want to deal with a crying Brighton before seven a.m. on a Sunday morning. Sundays are supposed to be *my* days.

She doesn't have time to respond, because it's our turn to order our everything bagels. She gets me an orange juice and for herself, a coffee with so much milk and sugar in it our dad would have asked her if she was planning on baking a cake with it. She's been trying to make herself like coffee all year and all of us have to pretend like she's not just trying to seem more grown-up than she is, or else she gets embarrassed.

Once she rolls the window back up, though, Brighton turns to me. She looks . . . proud, I think? I didn't realize having a crush on someone was worth being *proud* over.

"Yeah," Brighton says. "Like, if you had a crush on someone, you could tell me about it and it would stay between us. Mom and Dad wouldn't have to know until you were ready to tell them."

Well, if Brighton's giving me such a good opportunity for the experiment to progress, I'm not about to turn it down. We drive up to the window, Brighton grabs our bags and pays, and then, when we're on the road again, I speak up.

"Uh, yeah," I say. "So you saw me and Archie hanging out and put two and two together?"

Brighton stops too abruptly at a red light.

"Wait, what?" she asks. "Archie?"

I must look just as confused as she does.

"Yes, Archie?" I say, but it comes out like a question. "Who else would it be?"

Brighton takes that in for a second, and seemingly forces her face to relax out of the scrunched-up, questioning look it was just wearing.

"Sorry," she says. "I thought their name was something else, I guess. But, yay! Archie! That's exciting!"

For whatever reason, I don't buy her enthusiasm. Brighton *loves* sticking her nose in my business, and she knows all of my friends by name. She's even *met* Archie before, *and* said that he was cute! There's no way she didn't know who Archie was last night.

I don't have time to launch a full investigation into why Brighton's being so weird, because it's only another minute or two before we're in front of the shelter. I thank her for the ride and breakfast, gathering up my juice and bagel to make the dash under the awning, where Lydia's unlocking the front door.

"Hey!" she says, loudly so I can hear her over the rain, which has started to pick up even more. "I'm running late today, so could you feed the cats as soon as we get inside?"

That's the easiest question anyone's asked me in weeks.

"I'm gonna check on the rodent room," Lydia says a couple hours later, when all our chores are done and we're just sitting at the desk. "I'm eighty percent sure that hamster we got yesterday is pregnant."

Normally I'd immediately ask if I could come too. A pregnant hamster? I couldn't ask for better vet school preparation. But today, I can't quite shake the off mood I woke up with, so I let Lydia go ahead and pull my knees up to my chest on the big swivel desk chair.

My phone's been buzzing nonstop, which means Luna and Zoey and Jessa are all awake and messaging each other in our group chat. I don't really feel like catching up with all of those messages right now, though. Maybe it's the gloomy weather, maybe it's my weird conversation with Brighton earlier, or maybe it's my Thanksgiving realization, but I don't feel like myself. And if I can't be in a good mood in my favorite place in the world on my favorite day of the week, what am I supposed to even *do*?

I feel like something's brewing. Ever since my Thanksgiving epiphany, I can't stop thinking about what it would be like if there were someone in my life who was there for me the way Marcus was there for Brighton yesterday. If *that's* what Luna and Zoey have, then I finally get why they want to talk about it all the time. I've gone from trying my best to not pay attention to imagining every little detail of a relationship like that when I'm alone. I didn't even *want* to have one a couple of months ago! So clearly Archie's having some kind of impact on me. Heck, maybe I *do* like him. I've never liked anyone before, so maybe I just don't know what it feels like. Maybe

162

I've been feeling it this whole time.

Unfortunately, I think there's only one way to figure it out for sure.

I'm not *quite* ready to implement Step Six of my experiment just yet: that feels a little advanced. Besides, I only saw Marcus and Brighton hug; who knows whether I'd be so fascinated if I saw them kissing? (Actually, I know: hard pass to watching my sister and her boyfriend make out.) But I think I need to up the stakes a little bit. And, since today Jessa won't be at the shelter, it's the perfect opportunity to try to bring some more physical contact into the equation.

I gag, and it's not at the smell of the cat pee.

Even just thinking about it makes my stomach drop out of my body. But if I want what Marcus and Brighton have, that easy, comfortable feeling they give each other, this is almost definitely the first step.

The problem is, I have no idea how to go about it. I'd ask Luna or Zoey, but it feels like a big declaration. They seem to enjoy teasing each other about this stuff, like it's part of the fun. I'm worried that if I ask specific questions, they'll throw out hints and make things uncomfortable when we're all hanging out with Archie, and I think I'd barely be able to survive that.

I think I have to do this one on my own.

"Hey," Archie says, making me jump. Sometimes I forget that he actually exists outside of my brain, because real-life Archie and in-my-head Archie are completely different peo-ple. In my head, Archie is someone I'm going to want to kiss, someone who might become my first boyfriend. In real life, Archie is my friend who has a great dog and sends me extremely obscure music recommendations. The two of them don't seem to have a lot of overlap.

"Hi," I say. Archie gives me a funny look, and I realize it took me a really long time to reply to him. Oops. The inside-my-head Archie would find that extremely charming and cute, but real-life-friend Archie just laughs me off and starts scrubbing the litter box to my right. Again: objectively great boyfriend behavior, I think. There has to be *something* there.

"I know I said this yesterday, but thanks for having me last night," Archie says. "My mom asked me about forty million times whether I thanked you, so I decided I better double up so I can really make sure I did."

I smile with just one side of my mouth. "No problem."

"Hey," Archie says. He tilts his head around me to get right into my line of vision. "Are you okay? It must have been kind of weird to have everyone over when you're worried about, like, Halloween stuff."

I blink. It *was* kind of weird to have everyone over when I'm worried about, like, Halloween stuff. But I hadn't expected anyone to think about that.

This is basically what Marcus was doing with Brighton at Thanksgiving, right? She wasn't feeling her best and she talked to him about it and he helped make her feel better. That's what I was watching. That's what I wanted.

So maybe, gross as talking about feelings is, if I want

something like that with Archie, I could start now.

"Yeah," I say. "It's kind of hard to have stuff going on that I can't tell them about."

"Why can't you?" Archie asks. "I mean, shouldn't they be there for you no matter what? Isn't that, like, the whole thing with having friends?"

I laugh, but it comes out like a little huff. "I've heard that theory, yeah."

Archie raises both eyebrows at me, so I sigh again and keep going. "I know they love me, but sometimes they don't seem to get that we don't have everything in common. Like, they don't ever worry about money the way that my family does."

I mutter that last part. It's not exactly the coolest thing to admit, but Archie pretty much already knows everything.

"Yeah, I get that," Archie says. "I'm not exactly the top choice to hang out with when it comes to the guys we go to school with. Most of my best friends are online."

Huh. I actually didn't know that. All the guys in our class seem to just get along with each other in a way that, lately, seems way easier than how the girls get along (or don't get along, depending on who you're talking about). I hadn't considered that, actually, I don't usually see Archie hanging out with one specific group of people. He kind of drifts along, and everyone seems to like him, but no one seems to have taken him in the same way most other people have a spot.

"I'm sorry," I say, because it seems like that's the right thing to say.

He shrugs. "Don't think I'm miserable about it. It's just part of everything, sometimes."

I don't really know what he means, but he seems pretty sure of that, so I nod.

"Thanks for checking on me," I say, and then I realize what I have to do.

Slowly, like some kind of crush-obsessed sloth, I bring my arms up and, when Archie doesn't look repulsed at the idea of me, I take the plunge and wrap my arms around him.

The hug only lasts for a few seconds, but I spend the whole time internally cringing. It's not that it's *bad*, exactly; Archie's actually my friend now, and he did just do something nice for me, so it's not unreasonable to think that I might hug him for it. It's more that I'm thinking so hard about everything I'm feeling (or, specifically, *not* feeling) that it makes the whole thing seem weird.

I pull away and Archie smiles. I smile back, and then both of us get back to work on the litter boxes.

So, okay. That's twice now that Archie and I have hugged. I admit, the first time probably doesn't count as evidence in the experiment: a hug after apologizing for insulting him—even with flirty intentions—isn't the same as a *romantic* hug.

But *was that* a romantic hug?

I try to think about how I felt the first time Archie hugged me, last weekend. Relieved, mostly. When I realized how much I'd hurt his feelings, I also realized that I was starting to really like having him around as a friend. Knowing he didn't hate me was a massive weight off my shoulders, but it didn't feel anything like the way Brighton and Marcus's Thanksgiving hug looked.

I realize, annoyingly, that I might actually feel *less* during this hug than the one before it. I mean, sure, it's nice to hug a friend, but that's about it. I might as well have been hugging Luna or Zoey.

It's possible this mini-experiment was a bust. I mean, I felt more comfortable with physical contact when Jessa and I fell over yesterday. And *she's* certainly not going to be my boyfriend.

19.

World's Most Awkward Lunches

1. The last meal of a convicted murderer
2. The first time Brighton brought Marcus home and he had violent hiccups the whole time
3. This one, right now

Sometimes, things with my experiment seem impossible. If I think about it too hard, I start to feel a little ridiculous. Who do I think I am, trying to science myself into a relationship?

But other times, things just fall so perfectly into place that I *must* be doing something right.

When we're back at school on Tuesday, Archie comes to stand by my and Jessa's desks in homeroom.

"It's very important that you see this immediately," he says in an extremely serious voice. He pulls out his phone to show us the screen.

He swipes to a photo of Hank sitting on his couch. Well, *sitting* is kind of a loose term for it. It looks like Hank tried to do a somersault, but stopped halfway through. His butt is on top of his head, and he's looking at the camera like *I don't know how this happened either.*

"*Stop it,*" I say. "Oh my god, look at him!"

Then something extremely embarrassing happens: my eyes start to prickle.

"Are you *crying*?" Archie asks. He's half-horrified, half-amused.

"No!" I say. I wipe at my eyes roughly. "No. No tears actually fell, which means I didn't *actually* cry."

Jessa and Archie both give me the exact same *I'm not buying it* look.

"I just love Hank, okay?"

"That was so cute," Jessa says.

Ooh, great move. Saying I'm cute around Archie might make him start to think it, too.

Spurred on by Jessa's quick thinking (and also because I can't stop thinking about Archie saying he doesn't really have close friends at school), I decide to pounce on this opportunity. See? Sometimes things just line up.

"Do you want to have lunch with us today?" I ask Archie.

He blinks at me for a second. "Uh, sure?" he replies.

It's not huge enthusiasm, but I'll take it. It's possible it's a little jarring, because Archie only just got to class and also it's weirdly formal to ask him if he wants to have lunch with us. It's not like our friends ever exclude anyone—if anyone ever sat at our table we'd just talk to them like normal, as long as they were nice to us—so it's not like Archie needs an official invitation. But Halloween is fast approaching, and I don't think I can afford to waste much more time.

Enter the next step of the experiment: group hangs, school.

When lunch rolls around, I can't help but walk a little taller on my way to our table. Jessa's saying something, but I'm not really listening. I'm too busy imagining the looks on Luna and Zoey's faces when Archie comes to sit with us. In a few months, maybe he'll always sit with us. Maybe he'll put his arm around me and kiss me on the top of the head, the way Marcus did to Brighton when we all sat down for dinner yesterday.

That's the thing: I can imagine Archie doing all of these things and being this perfect boyfriend, but I think I might only have a crush on the Archie inside my head—every time I imagine a new scenario or moment between the two of us, everything goes dreamy around the edges—but I'm still working on it with the actual, real Archie who lives in the actual, real world. But the fact that I can imagine being Archie's girlfriend means I must be close to feeling it for real, right?

I'm kind of glad I can't talk to anyone about this plan. This whole thing has layers now, and I don't think I'd be able to explain it properly.

"NOAH."

Jessa's voice startles me out of my thoughts. I turn to my right, expecting to see her there the way she just was—the way she always is when we walk to lunch together—but instead there's just . . . cafeteria.

I look around. In hindsight, Jessa's voice *did* sound kind of far away. I just kind of figured that was because I was daydreaming.

She isn't to my right. She isn't in front of me. I spin in a slow

170

circle, trying to regain my bearings.

Oh god.

So, it's possible that I got so distracted by my own thoughts just now that I walked straight into the eighth-grade section of the cafeteria.

It's also possible I stopped directly in front of a table of very confused, very cool-looking eighth graders.

None of them are mean to me or anything. They look at me more like I'm a red panda at the zoo that fell out of a tree. Like I'm kind of cute but they mostly feel bad for me.

I wave (I have no idea why I wave. I hate myself for waving. But it happens before I can stop it) and scurry back to my normal lunch table.

Archie's already sitting down, so I don't even get to see what Luna and Zoey thought when Jessa told them I'd invited him to sit with us.

"Lost in thought?" Jessa asks. I don't know if it's just in my head, but she sounds grouchy.

"Yeah, I guess so." I shrug. I wouldn't even tell Jessa what I was thinking about, so there's no *way* I'd ever even hint at it with Archie around, too.

"We were just talking about Mr. Cross," Luna says. "I'm terrified of having him next semester."

Mr. Cross is known as basically the strictest grader in the entire school. A B from him is as good as an A+ from anyone else. Thankfully, he hasn't actually seemed as strict as everyone makes him out to be yet.

"Look at it this way," Jessa says. "You're friends with people who already have him. We can give you all our best Mr. Cross advice."

"Like the fact that he tries to wear fun ties on Fridays," Archie says. "He's never actually brought that up, but I feel like it says a lot about him as a person."

"Wait, he does?" I ask. Jessa looks just as surprised as I am.

Archie goes a bit red. "I'm the only one who noticed that?"

"Some of us can only dream of being that observant," Jessa says.

Archie looks kind of embarrassed, but I think being observant is probably a great quality to have in a boyfriend. Points all around.

"How's it going with Liam?" Jessa asks. Archie's shoulders relax a bit at the topic change.

Zoey scrunches up her face, completely distracted from the conversation we were just having. "I don't know, he's being weird lately. I asked if he wanted to FaceTime last weekend and he said that his parents were making him do homework, but then he posted a bunch of pictures from where he and his friends were hanging out."

"Red flag," Luna says. She talks like she's all wise now, like she's already been through life and she's waiting for us to figure it out. "He didn't want you to see who he was with? That can't be good."

"Maybe he just wanted to hang out with his friends." I surprise myself by speaking. "Like, maybe he felt bad about saying no to you, but he wanted to do something else, so he thought it would be easier to tell you he couldn't talk."

It's the first time I've really tried to join in on one of these conversations, and I don't think Zoey's realized that until now. She cocks her head at me.

"But that doesn't make any sense," she says. "It would be so much easier if he just told me what he was thinking. I wouldn't have cared if he just wanted to hang out with his friends."

"I never said it would make sense," I say.

Luna and Zoey laugh, and everything just fits so well like this, when I'm saying all the right stuff. It's not quite the same as it was before, but at least they're still here. At least I'm still part of the picture.

"So, Archie," Zoey says, leaning across the table. I feel myself go instantly pale. Oh god. What is she going to say to him?

It feels like an endless moment passes before Zoey says, "What color was Cross's tie today?"

I'd been holding my breath, but after Zoey asks that, all of it comes out in a relieved laugh. I take a sip of my water while Archie blushes again and explains.

"Usually they're just solid colors. Like, today's was just white. Very Brylee James."

From somewhere in the back of my mind, I watch in horror as I spit my water out clear across the table. I can't help it; I wasn't expecting Archie to say something like that and now I can't stop laughing.

"Sorry, sorry!" I giggle helplessly. I panic and try to wipe the table off with the hoodie I have stuffed in my backpack, but stop when Zoey gives me a moderately disgusted look.

"Oh my god, the Brylee James hate." Jessa rolls her eyes.

"It's deserved!" I say once I've calmed down. I take another sip of water and hope that Archie doesn't say anything else funny.

"Not you too," Jessa says to Archie. He laughs and shrugs.

"I learned from the best," he says, turning his head to smile at me. I smile back; even if I'm not in love with Archie, it never feels bad to be called *the best*.

"Ever since you brought it up, I can't unsee it," Archie says to me then. "I see all those stupid white houses and just wonder what cool stuff she destroyed inside of them."

"*Thank* you," I say. I try to give Jessa a smug, joking look, but she doesn't seem interested, which kind of makes the whole thing less funny.

Feeling extra bold, I reach out and grab Archie by the arm. I feel immediately flushed, and for a second I think, *Oh my god, it's actually starting to work*, but then I realize I think I'm more embarrassed at making a move in front of other people than I am in love with Archie or whatever. Either way, he doesn't seem disgusted or flinch away, so it can't have gone too badly.

"Last week, I saw an episode where she *smashed* a stained glass window. She didn't even try to save it!"

From the corner of my eye, I notice Luna and Zoey making Significant Eye Contact, which means they noticed the arm touch too. Good.

Archie makes a horrified face, and then Luna says something that makes him laugh and the conversation continues around me. I don't move my hand off of his arm until I notice the way Jessa's starting at it, and then I rip it away.

20.

Things I Wish I Cared More About

1. Luna and Blake
2. Zoey and Liam
3. Me and Archie

"Would you guys ever do a couple's costume?"

"Yes."

"Absolutely not."

Luna and Zoey answer me at the same time, and then all three of us laugh.

"I just think it's kind of like *ooh, look at us, we're a couple,*" Luna explains.

"That's *exactly* what I want it to be like," Zoey says. "Besides, Liam and I are already both actors, so we're used to both wearing costumes *and* attention."

It might be cheating to bring up something Brighton and Marcus were talking about a couple of weeks ago, but I figure if they're having conversations like this, it's something that people who've leveled up into the relationship game care very deeply about.

"All of you can enjoy your couple's costumes," Jessa says, picking absentmindedly through a rack of Halloween costumes from different decades. "I can't have anyone ruining my aesthetic."

"What are you going as this year?" Luna asks, and Jessa shrugs.

"I want to try and make my costume," she says. "So, like, whatever I can figure out how to do, I guess."

I instantly feel better about not buying anything from this shopping trip. I won't be the only one anymore. And, sure, maybe Jessa's only making her costume because it's fun and she wants to, and not because she *has* to, like me, but it still helps.

"Are you going cute or scary?" Zoey asks.

Jessa shrugs, so I interject.

"I'm going scary," I say. "The scariest thing I can possibly think of."

"Why do I feel like this is going to be some kind of ridiculous joke?" Zoey asks.

"No, I'm going as something seriously, seriously scary. You might have nightmares."

Zoey and I look at each other, but neither of us can stop ourselves from laughing. That's always been our problem. In first grade, we had to be separated because if we even glanced at each other we'd both dissolve into giggles.

"Zombie Brylee James," I say, and Zoey's full laugh explodes out of her.

"Think about it!" I continue. "Like, coveralls with blood all over them, and I've got, like, a ripped bandanna in my hair. Instead of *braaains* I'll be like *decorative graaaaass.*"

Zoey's folded over with laughter by the time I'm finished, and I'm not far behind her. Luna looks up and over at us questioningly, so Zoey goes over to explain the joke and I'm left with Jessa. For maybe the first time since we became friends, it's kind of awkward.

I've been trying to include Jessa in my conversations with Archie. I know what it feels like to not be included and the *last* thing I want is for Jessa to feel it too. But it's almost like now that there's a chance Archie likes me, Jessa wants to shut the whole thing down. Anytime I've tried to bring up The Plan since The Hug, Jessa changes the subject or squirms out of the conversation.

That's part of why I said yes when Luna asked if we all wanted to go costume shopping after school today, even though buying a costume is definitely not in the cards for me. For one thing, it's the Friday before a long weekend. All of us get carted off to family gatherings and dinners where we have to put our phones in baskets and whatever other pointless torture our parents subject us to on long weekends, which means Saturday sleepovers are pretty much off-limits.

"Are you okay?" I ask Jessa when Luna and Zoey are jokingly fighting over the last pink bob wig.

"What? I'm fine," Jessa says, but she doesn't quite look at me and she answers way too quickly, so she might as well have said *I'm not okay, please ask me many, many questions until I tell you exactly what's wrong.*

Thankfully, I don't even need to start with all of that,

178

because Jessa continues, "Seems like you and Archie are going pretty strong, huh?"

"Uh, I guess," I say. "I mean, I still don't really know what's going on, but I'm working on it."

I don't know why I feel the need to explain myself to Jessa—she knew that this was the plan the whole time—but there's something in the way she's standing and looking at me that makes me want to reassure her, even though I don't really even know what I'm reassuring her *of.*

"How *is* everything going?" Jessa asks.

I snort before I can stop myself. "What, is Archie in love with me because I've stopped actively insulting him when I try to flirt? Not quite. Honestly, the amount of effort Luna and Zoey are putting into this whole thing feels a little ridiculous."

Something lightens in Jessa at that, like she was carrying something heavy and she got to finally put it down. She smiles more openly than she has all week.

"I've never seen this much thought be put into a person someone else barely knows," she laughs. "The energy Zoey alone's putting into this could power a small country."

"Or the winter musical," I say. The cast list hasn't been posted yet, but Zoey's audition was incredible. None of us have any doubt that she'll be the perfect . . . whatever it is she was auditioning to be. Last year, she was a background character, and there's nothing "background" about Zoey.

"Noah?" Zoey asks, crossing the store to come and join Jessa and me. "Now that we're inviting boys to Halloween—"

I sigh. "Again, we have never had a Halloween party without boys being there."

"Yeah, but not *our* boys."

Our boys? I didn't realize I owned any boys. I picture myself returning Archie to the Boy Store. *No thanks, not quite right. Yes, I'll take store credit.*

"Isn't *your* boy going to be in Toronto?" I ask.

Zoey deflates slightly. "Yeah, but maybe we could find someone for Jessa!"

"Jessa's fine, thanks," Jessa says, saluting at Zoey from the other side of the clothes rack. I try to hide my smile but can't quite.

"All right, well, we can at least support Luna and Blake, right?"

I don't know how you're supposed to *support* a seventh-grade relationship between two people who've known each other their whole lives, but I guess that's another thing I'm supposed to understand.

"Yeah, of course," I say, like I have any idea what Zoey's talking about.

"Well, good," Zoey says. She glances behind her where Luna seems distracted by a heavily sequined costume and then whispers, "I think something's going on with her and Blake. Like, in a bad way. So I wanted to make sure they'd have time to actually hang out with each other."

"What's wrong with Luna and Blake?" Jessa asks.

"I just . . ." Zoey seems to debate whether or not to tell us, but clearly decides it's fine. "They've only kissed that one time, over the summer. And now it's been *months* and nothing. She doesn't know if he actually likes her or if he just wanted to kiss her that one time."

This might make me a terrible person, but the idea that Luna and Blake aren't actually a perfect couple makes me feel a bit better. Maybe if they aren't, me and Archie won't have to be either. Besides, if Zoey's distracted by Luna's drama, she won't have as much time to think about mine.

"We'll have to come up with a plan," I say. "To make sure he likes her."

Zoey's eyes light up. "Right? And then if he does, make sure he kisses her again."

My mind starts to run on super-speed.

"We should do it soon," I say. "Let's figure out what's going on with him so we can start the plan."

Zoey nods excitedly, and I smile at her even though an anxious swirl is starting to develop in my stomach. I'm pretty sure there are only so many plans I can keep straight in my head at once.

"Not this weekend, though," she says, a glint in her eye that immediately terrifies me. "I already have my own plan for *this* weekend."

Well, that doesn't sound horrible and menacing at all.

21.

Optimal Sleepover Activities

1. Lights-off hide-and-seek (with tackling)
2. Brownie night
3. Popcorn extravaganza

The Chius and I have an arrangement; I don't have to knock on their door, as long as they already know I'm coming. (They had to add that second part to the rule after the time in the third grade when I basically kicked their door down just as they were getting the call that Zoey's grandmother was dying. Not my finest moment.) So when Jessa and I make it to Zoey's house later that day, we breeze right in.

"Noah!" Mr. Chiu says when he sees us. "And . . . someone new! That hasn't happened in a while."

"Don't listen to him," I say to Jessa. "We're all very popular and cultured and have many, many friends."

"Oh, it's way too late to try to convince me of that." Jessa grins.

Mr. Chiu laughs, and I know Jessa's gotten his official seal of approval.

Jessa introduces herself, and then Mr. Chiu tells us Luna and Zoey are upstairs. We head up, and I feel a bit shiny and bright knowing that I'm the reason Jessa, this new person that everyone seems to love, is in our group now.

When we open Zoey's bedroom door, though, the vibe immediately changes.

"You *scared* me!" Luna says, from where she's apparently been pretty much pressed up against the door. I crane my neck around her to look into Zoey's room, only to see her peeking out from inside her closet. She darts her head back in, and I am deeply confused.

Luna tugs Jessa and me into the room, shutting the door firmly behind us.

"Liam called like an hour ago," she explains. "Zoey's parents don't know about him, so I've been standing guard just in case her dad comes upstairs."

Pretty sure the first thing they taught us when we got phones was to *not* have relationships with people that require hidden-away phone calls without the knowledge of your parents, but okay.

"She thinks they wouldn't let her go back to theater camp if they knew," Luna continues.

"So we're just going to sit here while Zoey has a full conversation without us?" I ask. It's one thing to feel like everyone's talking around you, but it's entirely another to have that be the actual plan for the night.

"No, romance hater," Zoey says, stepping out of her closet. "I cut the conversation short, just for you guys."

Oh, great. Now I'm *romance hater.* That makes me sound pleasant and approachable.

"Besides," Zoey says. "Once we figure out the perfect way

to break the news to my parents and introduce them to Liam officially, things will be fine."

"And how exactly do you see that going?" I scoff. "You'll just suggest a trip to Toronto and happen to run into him on the street?"

"That's one possible option, yes," Zoey says. "And where have you been, anyway? We've been workshopping this plan all week."

"Noah probably didn't notice the planning because she's been working on one of her own." Luna smirks.

"I told you already," I say. "Archie's going to fall in love with me all on his own; I don't need a plan."

"Okay, but you *do* need a kick in the butt," Zoey says. "It's been *months* since the summer and you guys haven't even kissed yet? I mean, don't think I didn't notice that arm grab at lunch the other day, but is that *it*? I don't want him to string you along like that."

Even though I'm not interested in this conversation *at all*, I can admit that it feels kind of nice to see Zoey going to bat for me like that. I know that if Archie *was* ever actually stringing me along, he'd have her to answer to.

"I don't think he's stringing me along," I say. "I mean, we hugged the other day."

Jessa drops her phone. It lands on the Chius' hardwood floor. We all wince in unison, but when she picks it up, the screen isn't cracked.

"Sorry," she says. She looks embarrassed, which I get; it's

184

always weird to go to someone's house for the first time when you don't feel comfortable there yet. Making a big noise like that probably didn't help. "Go on."

"*Yes*, go on, *Noah*," Luna says. "You and Archie hugged? When? Why?"

"He hugged me," I say. For some reason, that sounds cooler than me saying I hugged him, even though that's what happened. "At the shelter last weekend. He was thanking me for inviting him to Halloween decorating."

"Wait," Jessa says. "He hugged you at the shelter? Not just that one time at his house?"

Luna's eyes look like they're going to bulge out of her head. "You've hugged him *twice* and didn't think to tell us?"

"You were at his *house*?" Zoey adds.

"Jessa was there too," I say, feeling weirdly defensive about the whole thing. "It was after a shelter day. I helped him teach his dog a trick and he hugged me then, too."

It's kind of gross how quickly lies like that just pop straight out of me now. I absolutely cannot look Jessa in the eye knowing that she knows that was completely untrue. What if she thinks I'm making up the other hug? That would be so embarrassing, I think I might actually die.

"Well, that settles it," Zoey says. "You have to call him tonight."

I immediately go red—not because I'm nervous about talking to Archie, but because I know everyone's about to be staring at me and dissecting every word we say to each other.

For the most part, all of my conversations with Archie have been in private, or at least just around Jessa. There's so much less pressure there. Now, I know that even if this call lasts ten seconds, we're going to be talking about those ten seconds for the next ten *hours*.

"Look at her blushing!" Luna says, which makes me blush harder and also makes me want to claw off all the skin on my face.

"You're gonna do it, right?" Zoey asks.

I can think of *a lot* of things I'd rather do right now than call Archie (1. Step on a Lego. 2. Eat a slug. 3. Bathe a dog with worms), but if I say no now, they'll just spend the rest of the night begging me to do it.

I sit on Zoey's bed, surrounded by my friends. Archie picks up the phone pretty quickly, and I see Luna squeeze Zoey's arm. We haven't even said two words to each other yet and there's already something to discuss.

"Hey," Archie says. He sounds tired, so he's probably midway through another teen drama marathon.

"Hi," I say. "I've been instructed to call you by my friends."

"That makes me feel so special."

I laugh before I can help it. Zoey grabs my knee like I'm actively curing cancer by having this conversation.

"As you may know, it's a crime punishable by death if your friends tell you to do something at a sleepover and you don't do it," I say. "I had to save my own butt here. I'm sure you understand."

"So am I being *invited* to this situation, or are you all just dangling your friendship in front of my face?"

"The second one," I say immediately. I'd actually love it if Archie came to hang out with us for a bit, but I'd only love that if it were last year and we could all be normal.

"She misses you!" Zoey yells suddenly. My eyes go massive and I swat at her, but she's laughing too hard to notice.

I try to play it cool. "Yeah, I've been weeping for the whole twelve hours it's been since we've seen each other."

"Oh, same."

We wrap up the conversation quickly after that, because neither of us seems to have much else to say. I don't know if that's a good sign—like, we're so comfortable with each other we don't even need to talk—or a bad one.

"Okay," Luna says after I hang up. "I don't want to be mean, but I honestly didn't really get the whole Archie thing until now."

"Same!" Zoey shrieks. She and Luna are looking at me with matching expressions of near awe. Jessa's looking at me too, but she looks more thoughtful. "I wasn't sure if you guys, like, *had it*, y'know? But everything *flowed* so well! Even Liam and I still have awkward silences every so often, but you guys were perfect."

We were?

Huh.

"That plus your hug and you're well on your way," Jessa says. She smiles tightly at me and I squirm. I can't tell if that's her giving me her approval, or if there's something else she's not saying.

"Exactly!" Luna says. She seems totally oblivious to whatever Jessa may or may not be thinking. "You're going to have to teach us your *ways*, Noah."

I didn't realize I had ways. This is *very* interesting.

"Did you guys know that there's a *Rural Refresh* special that came out today?" Zoey asks, looking down at her phone with the browser open to a local news app.

We all whip our heads toward her.

"You let me go through all of that without telling me we had a prime hate-watching opportunity?" I demand.

Zoey opens her laptop and finds the *Rural Refresh* page on streaming. Brylee James's scary-big smile is hovering over the video like some kind of creepy god.

The episode is titled "Rural Refresh: New Beginnings," and I groan.

"'Brylee is on the move!'" Luna reads. "'Join her as she searches for the perfect family home in her beloved Middletown: the biggest Rural Refresh yet.'"

I pretend like I'm puking. "So she's *moving* here?"

Before, Brylee lived in the city and only showed up here when it was time to destroy a house. Now she's going to be here all the time? Just *around*?

"I bet she already has," Zoey says. "They film these so far in advance that she's probably just been wandering around without us even knowing."

"That's horrifying," I say.

"Just think," Luna says. "You've probably walked on the same road as Brylee James. You might have even touched something that she's touched."

Jessa starts coughing, choking on a popcorn kernel. I thump her on the back and it dislodges.

"What was that about?" I ask. "Too engrossed in this Brylee James ghost story to focus on chewing your food?"

Jessa gives me a tiny smile, her face dark red from coughing. "Basically," she says.

Zoey hits Play on the Brylee special, and I settle in, leaning my head on Jessa's shoulder. She still doesn't participate in our Brylee commentary, but I think she's okay, because after a while she puts her head on top of mine.

22.

Reasons to Have Friends

1. Someone will always tell you if you have food in your teeth and/or on your face
2. Good alibi in case you ever commit a crime
3. They'll ride it out with you if you tell them you're conducting an experiment on a boy to make him your boyfriend (special circumstances only)

Archie isn't at the shelter on Sunday.

I'm surprised that I'm as disappointed as I am, but I don't think I'm the right type of disappointed. Instead of being sad that I won't be able to see him and continue with the experiment, I'm more annoyed that after all the work I put into that phone call yesterday, I won't be able to reap any benefits.

"You look sad," Jessa says once Lydia leaves us to our tasks in the dog room. "Sorry you're stuck hanging out with just me."

At first, I think she's kidding, but then I hear the edge in her voice.

"What?" I ask. I know I could stand to be more eloquent here, but hearing Jessa sound upset with me for probably the first time in our entire friendship throws me enough that I don't know how else to respond. *Especially* because I don't know why she'd be upset with me.

"You know I never feel *stuck* hanging out with *just* you, right?" I ask, trying to make up for my *what*.

Jessa shrugs. "I mean, between you and Luna and Zoey and all your guy stuff, there doesn't always seem to be much room for me. And then you get here all mopey because Archie's not here and it doesn't seem too wild to think that maybe you're disappointed that it's just me."

She doesn't look at me when she says all of that, which means she doesn't see the way my jaw drops.

Are you kidding me? So all this time I've been trying to stop feeling like the odd one out, and in the process I've . . . made Jessa feel like the odd one out?

Knowing that Jessa's been feeling just as bad as I have the last few weeks makes something rotten sit in my stomach.

"I have to tell you something." It rushes out of me before I even give myself permission to say it. I mean, I could be blowing up the integrity of the entire experiment right now. Should I really give up on weeks of work just because Jessa seems a little sad?

But then Jessa looks up at me with big, vaguely watery eyes, and my brain goes, *BURN IT TO THE GROUND, TELL HER EVERYTHING IMMEDIATELY.*

"I don't like Archie," I say, and I watch Jessa's head shake, like the information just smacked her in the face.

"What do you mean you don't like Archie?" she demands. "Haven't we just spent weeks talking about how much you like Archie?"

Okay, so this part is a teeny bit . . . massively embarrassing.

I know my face is bright, shining red when I start to explain.

"So y'know how when school started, Luna and Zoey were talking about, like . . . *boys* a lot, and stuff?"

Jessa leans back away from me a little bit. She bites her lip and nods.

"I just kind of . . ." I don't know how to explain what it is I'm feeling—embarrassment and frustration and anxiety all rolled into one. "I've been pretending. To like Archie, I mean. Luna and Zoey have been so obsessed with their boyfriends, or whatever they're calling them, and I sort of panicked and when they thought I liked Archie I went with it. And I'm worried that they're going to see me as some kind of baby, because you have your own things going on and I'm . . . kind of getting . . . left behind."

I mumble the last part. I can barely look at Jessa, not wanting to see the look on her face when she learns that her cool camp friend has actually been an immature wannabe all this time. But when I peek one eye open, she's looking at me like she's waiting for me to keep going.

"So . . . you've been talking my ear off about how obsessed you are with Archie?" she asks eventually. "You know we could have, like . . . talked about anything else, right? I wasn't talking to *you* about boys. Why did you feel like you *had* to talk to me about them?"

I shrink down a little. That's the problem with Jessa: she always makes excellent points, even when they make me look bad.

"I guess I thought you probably felt the same way they did,"

I admit. "Everyone seems to right now."

Jessa rolls her eyes, but at least she's smiling now. "I told you guys I didn't have a crush on anyone *weeks ago*. Have you been secretly thinking that I was some immature kid that you wanted to leave behind?"

"No, but . . ." How do I explain to her that Jessa seems to understand the ins and outs of this way more than I do? That it seems like she isn't thinking about every little move she makes and every little word she says the same way that I do?

"But you're already cooler than us," I finish, pathetically.

Jessa rolls her eyes, but she doesn't seem upset with me anymore, which is a massive relief.

Now that I've actually told Jessa everything, I feel so much lighter. Before, keeping track of what she knew and how much and why was starting to feel like a full-time job.

But the fact that she's been feeling weird the same way I've been is just about the saddest thing I've ever heard.

"You don't have to worry, you know," I say to Jessa. She arches an eyebrow questioningly, so I continue. "About us."

Up this close, I can see all of the light little freckles across her nose and the way her throat bobs when she swallows.

"I'm not going to just forget about you," I say. "Like, if the plan works, and if Archie and I get together at the end of it? I won't leave you behind. I promise."

Jessa thinks about that for a really long time. I guess she's trying to decide whether I mean it or not, so I try to look really seriously into her eyes.

She breaks the eye contact first, turning her face away from me. Eventually, she takes a deep breath and then gives me a small smile.

"Sounds good," she says.

23.

Bad Omens

1. Stepping on cracks
2. Breaking mirrors
3. Your friends claiming to have boy-related plans

I know that it's a bad idea to go to next week's Saturday sleepover before I even arrive.

First of all, Archie's so busy doing whatever it is he's doing with his family this weekend that he hasn't texted me *once*. I know it's not reasonable to expect him to text me back right away when we aren't anything even close to dating, but it's still irritating.

Plus, Jessa can't come tonight, which means I won't have Jessa around to exchange secret looks with or to have my back if Luna and Zoey ask me too many questions about Archie that I don't know how to answer.

At the same time, though, I'm sick of not doing things because Luna and Zoey are going to be there. The whole *point* of the experiment was for me to keep hanging out with them! If this experiment makes it so that I don't want to see them, then it can't be working as well as I think it is. And I cannot accept that. So instead, I take a shower, stuff some clothes into my backpack, hug my parents, and walk to Luna's house.

Zoey's already here when I arrive, and she and Zoey each grab a hand and lead me up the stairs as soon as I step through the door. For a second, it actually makes me feel good. Normal. It reminds me of when we were little kids playing spies, and we had a top-secret mission Luna and Zoey needed to brief me on. By the time we make it into Luna's bedroom, all three of us are giggling breathlessly.

"What was all that about?" I ask. "Are we planning a heist?"

"Maybe next week," Zoey says. "This week, we're planning something even better."

"Better than a heist?" I raise an eyebrow.

"Okay, maybe not better," Zoey admits.

"What she's *trying* to say is: we're going to hang out with Blake and his friends at the park tonight," Luna says. She tries to sound cool and collected while she says it, but she's not fooling anyone. I can see, now, the nervous fidgeting in her hands and the way she's wearing an outfit that absolutely doesn't match, like she was trying on different outfits when I got here.

"I already asked my parents," Luna continues. "They're fine with it."

"And I assume they don't know who we're meeting at the park," I say.

Zoey laughs. "Of course not! That's why we're going to *this* park. We were going to go to the park near your house," Zoey continues. "But then we figured we don't want to get caught by anyone's parents. Y'know, just in case."

Zoey actually *winks* when she says *just in case*. I want to make a snarky joke like *what, just in case they see the fight club we started?* But I bite my tongue because I don't want to start off on the wrong foot.

"So we're going to walk to the park near school," Luna says.

Ugh. School's a twenty-minute walk away. That doesn't give me many options if this all goes sideways.

I feel bad as soon as I think it, so I try to compensate by throwing myself into helping Luna get ready. Zoey does her makeup (another new thing for me to try and get used to) and I give opinion after opinion about every single article of clothing in Zoey's wardrobe, which she's lending to Luna for the night.

"I don't want to bring the mood down," I say after the fifth shirt, "but I *do* feel the need to remind everyone that it is mid-October in Canada, and you'll probably be wearing a jacket the entire time you're outside."

Luna and Zoey look at each other and laugh.

"I genuinely didn't think of that," Luna says.

"What would we do without Noah?" Zoey asks.

"Get hypothermia, apparently," I deadpan, but I can't stop myself from grinning widely. That's all I've ever wanted to hear—that my friends love me and need me, even if I'm not doing everything they want exactly right. I hope they remember that they said that tonight. Ever since the summer, putting Luna in front of our guy friends has turned her into a different person. And that person doesn't always remember I exist.

Best-case scenario, we all get out of this without tears. Worst case, everyone ignores me all night because I don't know how to flirt.

Once we're all bundled up (and Luna has about thirty layers of lip gloss on, which seems counterproductive, since Blake doesn't seem like the kind of guy who likes wearing lip gloss, but I keep that particular observation to myself), we head to the park with the sun setting behind us. Luna's on her phone the entire time, texting Blake about our progress.

The guys are all at the park by the time we get there, leaning against swing sets and trying to look cool. They're laughing loudly, each one trying to outdo the other, and even though I've known them since kindergarten, it almost feels intimidating to look at them, yelling with the sun setting in the background so their shadows are huge and long and menacing.

Once we get closer, I make out everyone's faces. Blake's here, obviously, but so are all of his friends. Miles Duke and Callum McDonald, who have always been the loudest kids in our grade, and Jensen Douglas, who, actually, has always been really nice to me so I guess I don't mind so much that he's here. But still.

Blake and Luna hug once we're all together, and everyone makes some kind of little sound or comment about it. Both of them are blushing awkwardly when they pull away, which is really ridiculous because they don't normally act like that around each other.

"What are you guys up to?" Miles asks, swinging one-handedly from the monkey bars.

"We're at the park right now, Miles," Zoey says, and Miles rolls his eyes while the boys laugh at him.

"I meant, like, what are you guys doing this weekend?" he clarifies.

"I'll be at the animal shelter all day tomorrow," I say, because if everyone's going to ignore me tonight, I'm at least going to make it difficult for them.

"What, humans won't hang out with you?" Miles replies.

I scowl. This is exactly why I don't trust Miles; you try to have a normal conversation with him and he's mean for absolutely no reason.

But then I notice something. Miles quickly glances over his shoulder at his friends and Blake waggles his eyebrows.

Hm. A mean comment, delivered while smiling? In front of a crowd?

"Wait," I say. "Are you trying to flirt with me?"

The boys collectively lose it, laughing and *ooh*ing.

"Ice cold!" Blake says, but that's not even how I intended it.

Miles goes dark, dark red, and I wince. I didn't want to make him feel bad—I genuinely had no idea whether he was trying to flirt or not. I guess I have my answer now, though.

"You won't have any luck there," Zoey says with a smirk. "She's in love with someone else."

I resent the fact that Zoey used the word *love* when I've never suggested that was the case, but at least that'll hopefully get the boys off my back.

"Who?" Miles asks, hopping back onto the monkey bars like he doesn't care, swinging back and forth between a couple of rungs.

"Why would I tell you that?" I ask.

"Guess," Zoey says.

There it is. That *way* Zoey and Luna act now when we're around boys. Like they want to be the funniest, the loudest, the most important. And right now, it doesn't feel like they care about who they throw under the bus to do that.

"Or we could not do that," I say.

Obviously, no one listens to me. I guess I shouldn't have been worried that everyone was going to ignore me tonight; I should have been worried that I was going to be the entertainment.

Callum and Miles start shouting out names, and Luna and Zoey giggle and shake their heads with each name.

We only have so many guys in our grade. It's not going to be long before the process of elimination comes to end me.

"Stop," I say again. No one even acknowledges me, but I know if I say it any louder, I'll be the weird girl who's screaming for no reason. The one who can't take a joke. I try to make eye contact with Zoey or Luna, but neither of them is paying attention to me.

"Wait," Blake says after this goes on for a few minutes. He looks at me and cocks his head like a confused puppy. "It's not Archie, is it?"

Even though he doesn't sound like he's laughing at me, it still makes me blush hotly.

Luna and Zoey giggle even louder. They don't shake their heads. Callum and Miles join in on the laughter, but *they're* definitely laughing at me.

"You . . . get that that's not going to happen, right?" Blake asks.

Time stands still for a second.

At first, I'm sure I haven't heard him right. Like my brain has automatically conjured the worst-case scenario. But then Callum and Miles keep laughing, and Luna and Zoey are looking back and forth between me and Blake and it confirms it actually happened.

After that, the only thing I can think to do is run.

I bolt toward the school, running until I'm around the corner and at the front door where, on Monday, I'll have to go inside while knowing that everyone knows about Archie and, even worse, thinks there's no chance that he'd ever like me. I can hear Zoey yelling my name, but I don't turn around until I make it safely around that corner. I don't need anyone else hearing *anything* else from me tonight, thank you.

"Noah!" Zoey says one more time, and this time I whip around to face her.

"What was that about?" I demand. "You just *stood there!*"

Zoey looks surprised, which makes me even angrier. "I didn't tell Blake to say that. What was I supposed to do?" she asks.

I huff out a sarcastic laugh.

"You could have said *something*. You could have at least *tried*. You could have said *no, not Archie, someone else. Or* even just *not* turned me into a little game for the boys. You could have *been there for me*."

Zoey doesn't say anything.

"So what?" I continue. "You're just gonna stand here again? You're not going to apologize? You're not going do *anything* that might mean you're actually my friend and here for me?"

"What does it matter what Blake says?" Zoey finally asks. "He doesn't actually know if Archie likes you or not. He was just being annoying."

"No," I say. "Blake was being *mean*. Blake was being mean to me, same as the way Miles was mean to me. And you don't care, because you and Luna both think you're so important now just because a couple of boys decided to kiss you. It doesn't make you important, and what you just did makes you a bad friend."

Zoey looks angry now. "What, so now kissing Liam makes me a bad friend? How does *that* work?"

"It does when you decide that Liam kissing you is the only thing that matters!" I explode. "It does when you decide it's more important than our friendship. Do you think he actually cares about you? Do you actually think he's, like, in love with you or whatever? He's just some random guy that you barely even know. I'm sure he likes you just as much as the *real* girl-friend he probably has in Toronto."

I know that I'm being mean now, and that I just made a big deal out of one little comment, but I can't help it. It's like the

202

last month of planning and crying and worrying is all coming out of me at once, and it's not pretty. But I can't stop myself.

Zoey opens her mouth to respond, but I don't let her.

"I hope this was all worth it," I say. "Because it definitely wasn't for me."

I walk off, and this time, she doesn't try to stop me.

24.

Worst Places to Cry

1. In a public park
2. On a sidewalk
3. In front of your sister and her boyfriend

My parents have a rule that I can't walk by myself alone at night, which means I have two options: 1. waiting with the group until they decide to go back to Luna's house, or 2. calling Brighton for a ride home.

Obviously, I call Brighton.

"What's wrong?" she asks when she picks up, instead of saying hello like a normal person. Brighton thinks that every time someone calls her something horrible happened. Though I guess tonight she's right.

"Can you come and pick me up?" I sniffle. Oh. I hadn't realized I was crying, but it seems like realizing it makes it worse. My nose starts running and I can't quite catch my breath, so I actually stutter *can y-you c-c-come pick me u-u-u-u-up*.

"Where are you? What happened?" Brighton asks, panic coloring into her voice.

"I'm at school." I can't stop crying now that the floodgates have opened.

"How did you get all the way over there?" Brighton demands. "No, don't answer that. I'm coming, okay? Stay exactly where you are, I'll be there in, like, a minute."

It really is only a couple of minutes before I hear tires squealing and Brighton peels into the parking lot in our mom's van. I'm surprised I don't smell burning rubber, though with my nose running this much it's possible that I can't smell anything at all.

I feel a little better knowing that Brighton, at least, is willing to drop everything when I need her. She had to have been with her friends tonight, but she still came to get me the second I called her.

I'm starting to smile when I open the passenger door, but it freezes on my face once I realize someone's already sitting in my seat.

"Hey, Small Frye," Marcus says. "You okay?"

I don't respond to him. Brighton doesn't like it when I give Marcus attitude (that's how she says it, by the way. Like she's my mom), so I just huff and get in the back seat.

"What's wrong?" Brighton asks once I'm buckled in. "Do I have to kill someone? What happened? Where are Luna and Zoey?"

"Oh, they're fine," I say. "They're having a great time with all the boys who think I'm ugly and annoying and stupid."

Marcus and Brighton look at each other like they're wise adults and I'm their naive kid. It makes me so angry my teeth start to chatter.

"I'm sure they don't think that," Brighton responds eventually.

I roll my eyes. "Of course you'd say that. What difference does it make to you when you can go back to your real life where you're perfectly normal and have a perfectly normal boyfriend?"

"Having a boyfriend doesn't mean I'm *normal*," Brighton says. "You don't need a boyfriend to be normal."

"Cool," I say. "Thanks for imparting that wisdom. I'll keep it in mind when all of my friends stop talking to me because they've all decided that boyfriends are more important than friends."

"You don't have to be so snippy about it," Brighton says. Her patience can only last for so long when I'm in a bad mood.

"Y'know," Marcus says, "I don't think that your friends think boyfriends are more important than friends. I think they're probably just excited about something new. But eventually everything'll go back to normal."

"Shut up, Marcus," I say.

The car lurches to a stop. Brighton whips around in her seat to glare at me.

"Noah!" she yells.

"It's fine," Marcus says. "Don't worry about it."

"It's not fine!" Brighton says. "She can't be rude just because she's in a bad mood."

I slump down in my seat.

"Checks out," I say. "Picking your boyfriend over me. I guess I should be used to this by now."

"Oh, cut the woe-is-me crap," Brighton says. "I'm telling

you it's not nice to tell my boyfriend—or *anyone*, really—to shut up when he's just trying to be there for you. Do you need to go back to kindergarten and learn that lesson again or what?"

"It's really fine, Bee," Marcus says. I roll my eyes at him.

"You can just drop me off at home," I say. "I'll be fine, don't worry about me."

"I'm not worried about you anymore," Brighton says. "If you're okay enough to be a little goblin like this, you're fine."

I know I'm not making it easy to support me right now, but the fact that she doesn't even want to know about what happened makes me turn the corner from angry to sad.

"We were going to get snacks," Brighton pipes up, "but now that you've decided to act like a little kid, you can wait in the car like a little kid."

The store with the best snacks is just past our house, so I know she's being purposefully catty by driving right by instead of dropping me off. I roll my eyes when we pass by our house, and Brighton does an annoying little hair flip. Marcus is quietly sitting with his knees up to his chest like he's trying to make himself teeny tiny. That's fair.

"I'm taking the long way," Brighton says.

"I'm literally just sitting here," I snap back. "Do whatever you want."

Brighton purposely takes a wrong turn, driving onto an old, tree-lined street.

Ugh. I used to love this street. My mom and I would walk down it when I was little and she would point out all the old woodwork on peoples' railings, front doors, and shutters. Now, half of these houses are *Rural Refresh* houses. They all have the same black metal light fixtures outside. The same bland landscaping. The same white paint sloshed over beautiful old brick.

I count each *Rural Refresh* house as we drive down the street. One, then two, then three. This was one of Brylee's favorite season one spots.

"Stupid houses," Brighton mutters under her breath. At least we can agree on that much.

Brighton brakes at a stop sign while I glance out the window. We pass a *Rural Refresh* house and I roll my eyes. As if I could be any more upset right now.

Wait.

"Brighton," I say. "Don't drive yet."

"What?" she asks, and because she's confused she doesn't drive forward, so I don't explain anymore.

When I look at the house again, I realize it's Brylee's Middletown Dreamhouse. That's what they kept calling it, like she was Middletown Barbie. The old brick painted off-white, the black window trim (I guess she decided to mix things up for her own house), the sparsely landscaped garden that she ripped massive rosebushes out for. This is Brylee's house. She's probably in there right now.

As if the universe is reading my mind, the front door opens just as I have that thought. I duck down in my seat slightly, but as soon as I see a blond head come out of the house, I straighten up.

The person—the girl—taking the trash out has a familiar blond ponytail. She's wearing a familiar tie-dyed shirt, and when she turns around to go back inside, I see the familiar name of my camp on the back. Everything about her is familiar, in fact.

She moved here because her mom got a job. She never wants to laugh at Brylee James with us.

Oh my god.

I watch Jessa walk back into her stark white house, and Brighton drives off.

25.

Things I Can Do Now

1. I don't know
2. I have no idea
3. No clue

I don't know what to do.

On Sunday morning, Luna tries to text me, and I ignore her messages. Tellingly, our group chat doesn't ping at all. I can just picture Luna and Zoey talking about me in their own chat thread.

Brighton tries to talk to me a couple of times, but I only speak to her when I absolutely have to. I know that, technically, she didn't do anything wrong. But it still feels like she picked Marcus over me last night, and I'm kind of sick of people choosing other people over me.

I want someone to pick me.

And then there's Jessa. I'm not too proud to admit that when I got home last night I cried in my room for a really long time. I know I shouldn't feel like this, but realizing Jessa is *Brylee James's daughter* has utterly blown my mind.

Not only does Jessa live somewhere that might as well have a neon sign on the door that says *I HATE MIDDLETOWN'S*

SMALL BUSINESSES, she also didn't trust me enough to tell me who her mom is. Did she even see me as a friend? Is this just another time when I've been more excited about a friendship than the other person?

And what about Jessa? All this time I've been making fun of her mom in front of her and she's never said anything. It feels like a punch in the throat every time Luna and Zoey casually bring up spending money in a way that I *know* I'd never be able to do, but at least they don't know what's going on with my family. Has Jessa been feeling the same way around me all the time?

Don't get me wrong: I still hate *Rural Refresh* and I still think Brylee James needs to leave us all alone, but if Brylee *had* left us alone, then I guess Jessa wouldn't have moved here in the first place.

Ugh, I've made my first new best friend since I was practically a baby and I have *Brylee James* to thank for it? This just gets worse and worse.

When I get to the shelter on Sunday morning, my goal is to avoid every possible interaction with every possible person. Jessa doesn't know that I'm upset with her, and I'm not in the mood to explain it. I'm self-aware enough to know it doesn't make logical sense. And I *really* don't want to see Archie.

There's no way Blake didn't tell Archie about what happened on Saturday. Or if he didn't, Callum or Miles would have. It's exactly what I suspected before: if the wrong person knows who you like, it'll spread to the whole school in a couple of hours. I'm sure Archie got the whole story. Not only does weird Noah like him, she also freaked out on all his friends and made everyone uncomfortable.

Great.

"Can you make it so that I do literally anything that means I don't have to talk to anyone else today?" I ask Lydia. Even though it's starting to get really cold in the mornings, I convinced my parents to let me ride my bike to the shelter this morning so I could make absolutely sure I'd be the first one here.

Lydia looks at me for a second. Assessing, the same way Brighton does, but I don't mind it as much because I know she'll give it to me straight and there's a pretty decent chance that she won't tell my parents unless she thinks I'm, like, gonna go rob a bank after this or something.

"You look like crap," she finally says. If I were in a better mood, I'd probably think that was funny.

"I trust that you have a lot of people in your corner," Lydia continues. "So you don't have to talk to me about it if you don't want to. But you should know that you *can*, if you do want to. Maybe I could provide a . . . different perspective."

"It feels like everyone has the same perspective right now, actually," I say. I know nothing that's gone on the last few days has been Lydia's fault, but I still bristle at the thought of yet another person not understanding how I'm feeling. I thought Jessa got it, but it's become more and more clear that she doesn't. I don't know if I have it in me to try and make someone else understand.

"I might surprise you," Lydia says. "Try me."

I don't say anything, looking down at my hands. Lydia waits for a minute and then speaks again.

"We can go into my office, if you want?"

I don't know if I want to turn this into a Talk, but if we're in Lydia's office then when Jessa and Archie get here I won't have to see them, so I get up and lead the way.

Lydia shuts the door and sits behind her desk. She gestures for me to sit on the uncomfortable seat across from her. And the second I do it, I start to cry.

Lydia doesn't say anything. She lets me cry it out for a bit. She doesn't seem to think it's weird or annoying when I open my mouth to try to explain myself and then end up just burying my head in my hands again. I think this cry's been building up since the day I got home from camp, and I'll just have to ride the wave until it's done.

When I finally feel like I can get words out without sobbing, I peek up and see Lydia's set a box of tissues in front of me. I laugh wetly and grab a few to start cleaning myself up.

Then I say what's been running through my head the whole time I've been crying.

"I don't think I have any friends."

Lydia doesn't look convinced about that, but it's still how I feel. Saying it aloud makes me feel about a million times worse.

"Jessa and Archie don't *have* to wake up at the crack of dawn to come and volunteer with you," she says. "And I'm sure your other friends would disagree too."

I shrug, looking away. "I don't think Jessa likes me as much as she said she did. She doesn't trust me. And my other friends caused the most embarrassing moment of my life yesterday just so that they could seem cool to a bunch of boys."

Lydia tries to stifle a laugh at the way I practically spit the word *boys*.

"I just feel alone," I admit. "And I never used to. But I do now. All the time, it seems like. Even when my friends *are* around. Even when things are going well with them. I just feel like I'm far away and they don't know how to reach me. And I don't know how to reach them."

Lydia nods like that makes perfect sense, which is very nice of her because it barely made sense to me.

"If your feelings are different from your friends' feelings, it's easy to feel like you aren't connected to them," she says. "I don't think it means that you're alone, but I've felt lonely like that before too."

"It scares me," I say. "I don't want to keep feeling like this. I just want things to go back to the way they used to be."

"I get that," Lydia says. "I mean, if you're feeling lonely, of course you'd want to go back to feeling not lonely."

". . . There is no way there's a *but* to that sentence, come *on*."

Lydia can't stop the laugh that bubbles out of her. "Sorry, kid. Of course you'd want to go back to feeling not lonely, *but* sometimes that feeling is something that happens when you grow up. You learn more about yourself and you learn that you aren't the exact same person you used to be, or that you aren't the exact same person as your friends. And if they're good friends, you learn that it doesn't matter."

"There are things that are *so important* to them now that don't matter to me at all," I say. "I can't even pretend to care about them."

Lydia nods slowly. "You don't always need to care about the same things your friends care about. You just need to care about *them* as people. Have you been doing that?"

I don't have to think about it very hard to know that the answer is no. I've been so afraid of losing Luna and Zoey that I haven't even realized I haven't done much to . . . y'know, keep them.

"I've been trying to make them want to stay friends with me," I say. "But it's . . . possible that was more about me than them."

"I know that you're a good person," Lydia says. "No one who cries as often as you do in an animal shelter could ever be a bad person. But you're growing up. And when you do that, you change. And when you do *that*, you and your friends almost always become different people. You get to decide whether you still want them in your life, but even when you do, things can still get messy. This is just the first time you have to learn how to do that."

"I don't want to," I say. I know it comes out like a little kid, but it's true.

Lydia hesitates for a second, looking at me with that same searching expression she had before we came in here.

"I used to feel a lot like you, I think," she finally says. "I used to feel really lonely, too."

"Even with friends?"

She nods. "Sometimes especially with friends. When I was your age, when I was growing up? It could feel like no one felt the way I felt. Especially when my friends all got older and their interests seemed to all be the same interests. And then I was just sort of . . . there."

My jaw nearly drops. "That's it *exactly*! That's so wild, I can't believe you felt that too."

"It's more common than you think," Lydia says. "And it takes a lot of thinking about yourself and what you value and what you want out of life, but I promise that eventually you'll figure all that out, and then you'll know what'll help that lonely feeling go away."

"You're very wise," I say to her. I mean for it to come out as a joke, but I'm kind of serious.

Lydia scoffs. "I don't know about that. I just know a lot about this kind of thing. Most of my friends have had similar experiences growing up too."

"Where do you find friends who all had the same issue?" I demand. "I want some of *those* friends."

There's that face again. Weighing something up. Watching me carefully.

"Well," she says slowly. "It's a pretty common experience for queer people. Most of my friends are queer, like me, so we have a few shared experiences."

Something thuds in my chest, and I realize it's my heart. It's suddenly beating faster than I've ever felt it beat before. Faster than gym class sprints. Faster than camp swimming races.

"So that's something that . . . that . . . people . . . all go through?" I ask. I can barely hear myself over my pounding heart.

"Not necessarily," Lydia says. "I don't think that's an exclusively queer thing. It's just something that people in that community feel sometimes. But feeling it doesn't mean that you're queer, and not feeling it doesn't mean you're *not* queer. Does that make sense?"

"Sure," I say. "But do you . . . do you think that that's the reason *I* feel that way?"

Lydia purses her lips.

"Well, how did you feel when I said it?" she asks. "Is it something you've ever considered before?"

"No," I say right away. It's true. "Me and Luna and Zoey have always been exactly the same. The Three Musketeers and all the other corny stuff our parents say, y'know? We all went through our doll phases and our video game phases and our dance video phases at the same time. I just assumed that I would be the same as them all the time. In everything."

Lydia nods. "It's hard to know something about yourself when no one ever tells you that it's an option."

But someone's telling me it's an option now.

"You don't have to tell me anything you're thinking," Lydia says. "And you don't have to have any big realization or make any kind of declaration unless and until you feel like it. But you can always realize or declare stuff to me. Really, any kind of crap, promise."

I laugh, but my mind is racing.

A scientist is supposed to consider all angles of an experiment. Vets are supposed to check on every possible option before making a diagnosis. So why didn't I consider this before? It's not like I didn't know gay people existed before this moment, it's just that I'd never met one in real life. (Though I guess that's not actually true, considering what Lydia just said to me.)

Lydia leaves the office, saying I can sit and think here for as long as I need. As glad as I am that she talked to me today, I'm happy she's leaving me alone for a bit. It's all a bit much to process.

I think about what Lydia said to me, the question I didn't answer. *How did you feel when I said it?*

I don't know if was the feeling of a great realization, or just panic that I hadn't considered something in my experiment, but it was *something*. It was a feeling I can't quite describe, something high-flying and heavy all at once.

But I'm a woman of science. Further research is required.

26.

Experiments I Would Rather Do Today

1. How quickly do piranhas eat human flesh?
2. Effects of skinny dipping in a Canadian lake in late October
3. How loudly can a person pass gas in school without being noticed?

I find Archie quickly once I leave Lydia's office. I made sure to check my reflection in my phone's camera to make sure I don't look too much like a drowned rat after my minor breakdown, so we're good.

Archie's alone, which is perfect. I still don't actually know where I stand with Jessa, but if it's true that she *does* value our friendship as much as I do, then she's probably pretty confused about why I haven't texted her back all weekend. I don't want to have to explain all of that quite yet. Not until I have answers, anyway.

But that means actually *getting* the answers.

I haven't had much luck with my crush experiment, but I've always been a hands-on learner. Maybe I don't like boys at all, like Lydia suggested, or maybe my brain just needs something to kick it into gear.

I'm proposing a mini-experiment. I don't have the time to write it down and record my findings, but I'll just have to trust that I'll remember.

Step One: determine whether Archie knows about what happened yesterday, and, subsequently, whether he thinks I'm a loser or not.

Step Two: engage original Step Seven: kissing.

I feel like I'm going to throw up when I walk into the rodent room, and for once it's not because of the smell of rat pee. I'm kind of hoping that when I open the door and see Archie standing in my favorite place, working at something that means a lot to me, something will change. But nothing seems to.

Maybe if we kissed, I'd start to feel it.

"Hi!" I say. I try to sound excited but not too excited to see him.

"There you are," Archie says. "Are you and Lydia involved in some kind of *scheme*? You've been in her office for ages."

"Sorry for not gracing you with my presence earlier," I say. It's much easier to give flirting another chance when I'm in a good mood. And I'm *definitely* in a good mood now that Archie's talking to me like he has no idea what happened. He was with his family all day, so maybe I've made it to him before any of the boys could tell him anything. Suddenly, I'm not so annoyed at him not texting me all day yesterday. Even if it turns out I don't like him at all, it's a relief that he never has to know how badly I was embarrassed. I walk right up to him so that we're face-to-face. Kissing distance.

"It's been very difficult," Archie deadpans. "But mostly because I've been scrubbing hamster cages for the last half hour, and they're surprisingly difficult to catch when they wiggle away."

Maybe it's better to just not overthink this. I squeeze my eyes shut, purse my lips, lurch forward, and . . .

. . . Get hit in the forehead by Archie's hand.

"Noah," he says. "I need to talk to you."

Oh my god.

Oh my *god*, this is so embarrassing that I don't even know how I'm going to survive another minute. I actually, genuinely, seriously think I might just evaporate right now.

"Maybe I should just go," I say. What I *want* to say is *maybe I should just move to Alaska.*

"Why?" Archie asks, as if he didn't just witness the single most humiliating thing anyone has ever done in the history of the universe.

"What do you mean, why?" Tears are starting to prickle at the corners of my eye. Oh, great. Let's make this whole thing even better by me starting to ugly cry. "That was pretty much the most embarrassing thing imaginable."

"You don't need to be embarrassed," Archie says.

I snort. "No, I think it's pretty obvious that I do, in fact, need to be embarrassed."

"Maybe I could see being embarrassed if you actually liked me," Archie says. He smirks a little, raising an eyebrow.

"What do you mean?" I demand. "Of course I like you!"

Archie crosses his arms. "All right," he says. "If you can name one *genuine* reason why you like me, I'll kiss you. And, because I'm being nice, I'll ignore the fact that when I just said I would kiss you, you made a face like someone farted."

As *if* I'd be that unprepared.

"You're always nice to people, even if you don't hang out with them," I say. "The other day, when Callum stole Sofia's pencil case, you got him to give it back to her. You didn't tell anyone when I told you about my family's money stuff."

Archie looks at me carefully. "Right, but . . . do any of those things make you want to *kiss* me?"

I sputter for a little while, but Archie's got a point. Hm. Noted.

"Not . . . exactly," I admit.

"Not at all!" Archie laughs. "So what on earth have you been *doing*?"

It doesn't take too long before I'm laughing with him, and I think, *At least I still have this.*

It only occurs to me just then that Archie is one of my best friends. I guess I was so focused on him as the subject of the experiment that I didn't realize what was right in front of me all along. I'm just as happy to see him as I would be if he were Luna or Zoey.

Or at least Luna and Zoey from last year. Or even last *week*, before yesterday.

If Archie's one of my best friends, I guess I can trust him with the details of my experiment. Or, well, not *all* of the details. I might not like Archie romantically, but that doesn't mean it wouldn't be embarrassing to tell him every little bit of what I've been thinking for the last couple of months.

I take a deep breath and decide to give Archie a rough outline of what's been going on in my brain. The way Luna and Zoey seemed so mature and different when I returned from camp, the way I've been feeling left behind and left out and lonely. I even share the embarrassing thing Blake said to me on Saturday. To my absolute horror, by the time I get to the Blake part, tears are starting to roll down my cheeks.

"Ugh, sorry," I say, wiping at my face roughly. "It's just that I kind of thought Blake was my friend too, y'know? So the fact that he was *so sure* that no one was going to like me like that kind of hurts."

Archie's face falls. "Oh no," he says. "That's what you thought he meant by that?"

I snort. "It's kind of difficult to figure out what else he might have meant by *that's not going to happen.*"

"Oh man," Archie's rubbing his hand over his face. "Noah, I'm *gay.*"

My brain freezes for a moment.

"Wait, what?" I ask, because I can't think of anything else to say.

Archie laughs, and then covers his mouth like he feels bad but couldn't help it. "I'm sorry!" he says. "I thought you *knew*! Everyone knows!"

"Clearly everyone does *not* know!" I sputter indignantly.

"Noah. Even *Lydia* knows."

"*Lydia?* My Lydia?"

"I complimented her on the *very large pride flag* she has in the shelter lobby!"

Huh. He did do that.

I bury my head in my hands and laugh. "Oh my god, I forgot about the pride flag."

"I really have not been trying to keep this under wraps," Archie says. "I'm almost offended. Should I wear more rainbows?"

"I don't think it would have helped," I laugh. "I didn't even know that Lydia was gay until about twenty minutes ago."

Archie blinks at me.

"I truly love and value you as a friend, but that is the wildest thing I've ever heard."

"It's not like she's super out there with it!" I exclaim. "I've known her for years and this is the first time she's said something to me."

Archie tilts his head at me. "I mean, not to stereotype or anything here, but she has short green hair, she flies a pride flag in her place of work, and, oh yeah, she's mentioned her girlfriend in every conversation I've ever had with her."

I throw my head back and groan. How could I have not put two and two together? I've been even more self-absorbed than I thought. "I thought she meant it like the way some adults are like *hey, girlfriend!* I didn't know she meant *girlfriend* girlfriend. My mom calls her friends her girlfriends all the time!"

I'm expecting Archie to make fun of me. If I were Archie,

I'd make fun of me. But instead he just shrugs and says, "Well, now you know."

I just look at Archie for a minute. He's been here the whole time, and I didn't even realize how glad I was about that until just now.

"Can I hug you?" I ask.

He laughs. "Only if it doesn't become part of an *experiment*."

I laugh and open my arms, giving him a massive hug. It sounds ridiculous, but Archie coming out to me is a huge weight off my shoulders. Hearing him say he's gay made something click in my brain, like *yes, that's who he is*. Maybe my experiment did actually work, just not the way I initially expected. Maybe I needed it to find Archie (and keep Hank in my life, obviously).

"Noah?" Archie asks into my shoulder.

"Yeah?" I ask into his.

He pulls away slightly to look at me. "Were you seriously trying to have your first kiss in the *rodent room* of the animal shelter?"

27.

Best Possible Outcomes of My Experiment

(Ranked from least to most optimal)
1. Everything goes according to plan, no embarrassment occurs
2. Some embarrassment occurs, but things work out
3. This one

"Okay," I say after Archie's finished laughing at me and making jokes about movies featuring talking rodents at my expense. "If we're friends now, can I tell you a secret?"

"First of all, I was under the impression that we've been friends this whole time," Archie says. "You're the one who was actually using me as a scientific experiment."

I wince. "That's . . . fair."

"Second of all," Archie says, "yes, obviously immediately tell me all of your secrets."

I grin. "Okay, but this is, like, a *big* big secret. You really can't tell *anyone*."

"I don't know who I'd tell, but sure."

I don't actually know if Jessa is here, but if she is I think Lydia might be keeping the two of us separate, because she hasn't come in to say hi even once. I'm sure Luna and Zoey have already told her everything that happened the other night, so even if I *had* any interest in speaking to her, I don't think it matters anymore anyway.

Either way, I look around just in case before I whisper, "Jessa's mom is Brylee James."

Archie brings a hand up to his chest and gasps dramatically. "Oh my *god*!"

My shoulders slump. "You *knew that already*?"

So Jessa could tell Archie, a guy she's only known for a few weeks, but she couldn't tell one of her best friends?

"She told me after that day I sat with you guys at lunch," he confirms. "When we were laughing at Brylee."

Ugh, another reminder that I've been a terrible friend to Jessa. Exactly what I need.

"Wow, I'm a horrible person." I sit down on the floor and a rabbit inches up in her cage to sniff me.

"I mean, she told me she's also not the biggest fan of her mom's design work, if that helps," Archie says. "But yeah, you definitely messed up there. Turns out it kind of sucks to have your best friend constantly tell you your mom is some kind of devil woman from the underworld."

I cover my face with my hands.

"Why didn't she *say anything*?" I'm almost dizzy with the way everything's turned around so quickly. I came into the shelter this morning wanting Archie to be my boyfriend and never wanting to speak to Jessa again.

"I guess she didn't want to rock the boat," Archie says. "I mean, you were her first and best friend here."

I peek at him from behind my hands. "Does she hate me?"

Archie gives me a sarcastic look that I can't really decode, and then snorts. "Obviously not. I mean, you hurt her feelings, but she also knew you didn't know that Brylee was her mom. It's not like you knew and kept doing it anyway. She told me she was pretty sure she could hide who her mom is for long enough to convince you that Brylee isn't that bad."

The thing is, I still think, *But she* is *that bad*, immediately. Even though Brylee James is Jessa's mom, she's still destroying all of my favorite houses. She's still bringing city people who brush past you in the street and don't think you're worth their time or attention to Middletown. And she's still the person who, whether she means to or not, is practically putting my parents out of business.

"Oh my god, are you seriously going on some kind of *Brylee James sucks* rant in your head right now?"

I blink at Archie's bewildered face. Huh. I guess as much as I've been observing him, he's been observing me. Though I guess that could just be that we're friends now.

"Everything that's going on with my family right now is basically Brylee James's fault," I say in my defense. "She's the reason people aren't hiring my parents for stuff anymore."

Archie shakes his head. "I'm pretty sure if it wasn't Brylee James, it would be someone else. Towns get bigger all the time. If a bunch of city people want their houses to look boring, and Brylee will make them look boring, that's not exactly a crime. It's her job."

Hm. Sure, Brylee is the main reason Middletown's becoming so popular, but actually, if I really think about it, city people have been coming here for as long as I can remember. They built their cottages by the lake and they spent their summers making everywhere busy and then they left. Except not all of them did. Every year, more and more of them seemed to stay. And those people probably always wanted someone like Brylee to come along and . . . y'know, *refresh*.

"You don't have to like it," Archie says. "But the people are here to stay, and Brylee's always going to be Jessa's mom."

I cut my eyes at him. "I don't need you being wise when I'm trying to have complicated feelings. That's very rude."

"Sorry, I can't turn it off. All wise, all the time."

"If you were so wise, you would have told me all of this ages ago and I could have figured it out by now," I grumble.

Archie snorts. "Yeah, I guess I'm not wise *all* the time. Like, when you said you had a secret, this was *not* what I thought you were going to say."

The same feeling I had in Lydia's office earlier comes over me. I'm hot and cold at the same time, kind of tingly around the edges.

"What did you think I was going to say?" I ask.

Archie looks caught out, like he didn't mean to say anything at all.

"Nothing," he says. "I just didn't think it would be about Brylee James."

"Did you think it was going to be about me?"

It's like scratching a mosquito bite: I have to keep doing it, even though I'm not sure if I'll be happy with the end result.

Archie eyes me suspiciously. "Maybe," he says. "Why, do you have a secret about yourself?"

And that's the equivalent of the mosquito bite starting to bleed. I may be in over my head now.

"I don't know," I say, shrinking back. It was fine talking *around* what I've been thinking in the back of my head since I spoke to Lydia, but I don't know if I'm ready to actually say it out loud.

"I might," I add. "But I don't know for sure yet. And it feels like I should know for sure, right?"

Archie shrugs. "I knew I had a secret pretty much as long as I can remember, but that doesn't mean *you* have to know if you have one."

Okay, let's think about this objectively. Scientifically. I was just about to kiss Archie to try to see if I liked boys at all. Archie's just one boy, so my sample size was *way* off. But then again, it's not like Archie kissed every girl in the world to find out that he was gay. I think I would have remembered that.

"So it's just . . . a feeling? Just something you know?" I ask.

"For me, yeah. I haven't had a chance to ask all of the other gay people in the universe yet, but I'm working on it."

Now that he's actually said what we're talking about, I feel a little more confident. We're talking about secrets, but it's not really a secret for Archie, is it? And if it's not a secret for Archie, maybe it wouldn't have to be a secret for me. Maybe it could just be a part of me.

Because I don't know about all the other boys in the world, but I *definitely* don't want to kiss Archie. And I can't think of a time when I swooned along with Luna and Zoey about a famous boy they both loved. But I *can* remember how I've watched *terrible* movies just because an actress I've liked is in them. I've gotten angry at my mom for not *getting* how cool I think some singers or models or whoever are. And when I think about how I feel imagining kissing that blurry boy-blob compared to a blurry girl-blob, it's . . . definitely different.

"I think I might have something to tell you?" I say. I barely squeak it out, but Archie grins like that's the best thing he's heard all day.

"I'm all ears."

28.

Halloween Misconceptions

1. Black cats are bad luck (don't even get me started)
2. Full-size candy bars are the best (the mini ones taste different!)
3. The day has to be scary

Y'know that feeling when you wake up on Christmas morning, or your birthday, or some other special day, and it feels like even the air is special? Like everything somehow knows that that day is important?

That's usually how I wake up on Halloween. My parents make pancakes in the shape of ghosts and garnish them with fun-size chocolate bars, and then we put on our costumes and head out for the day. In the evening, the Fryes host our annual Halloween party and pass out candy to trick-or-treaters.

I don't know if this Halloween is going to be the same as all the ones that came before it. I mean, can you even have a Halloween party if your two best friends don't want to come to your house? Probably not. Plus, last year Brighton said she didn't want to wear a costume to school anymore, and what's the point of doing our normal Halloween morning if I'm the only one fully invested?

But when I wake up on Halloween morning, before I even open my eyes, I start to feel the first little twinkle of the Halloween Magic start to spark in the back of my head. So what if maybe my friends won't want to come over tonight? I can always pass out candy. One of the best parts of Halloween is seeing all the tiny little kids in their costumes. Plus, the last time I checked, my parents don't say, *So, how many friends do you have?* before they dole out the ghost pancakes.

I roll over in bed and my eyes flutter open. There's an extra special coziness to the quilt I'm under, to the fan gently spinning overhead (I reject the idea that a light breeze is something that should be reserved only for summer), to the demonic presence standing at the end of my bed watching me sleep . . .

Uh, excuse me?

I blink fully awake and realize someone's standing in my room, watching me sleep. I scream. And not a cute, girly scream either. The scream of a grown adult. The scream of a grown adult who's already seen the horrors of the world, and thus knows that this is the worst of them all.

The person at the end of my bed rushes forward when I don't stop screaming, shoving their hands over my mouth. Just in case I wasn't already having the morning from everyone's worst nightmare.

"Noah!" the figure says. I blink the figure into focus and realize who it is and shove Zoey's hand off my face.

"You *promised* you'd stop doing that," I say. I'm still breathing heavily but I manage to scowl at Zoey.

"Well, *you* promised to be friends with Luna and me forever, and then you decided you hated us overnight out of nowhere, and *then* you stopped talking to us, so drastic measures had to be taken."

I don't say anything for a while. I want to tell her that I don't hate her and things can go back to normal like nothing's changed. But whether I like it or not (and I don't), things *are* different. Zoey has a boyfriend and I don't. Zoey likes boys and I . . . maybe, probably, don't. Sometimes it feels like this could be the beginning of the end of us.

"I didn't exactly decide it out of nowhere," I say. "I decided it when you and Luna threw me under the bus to try and seem cooler in front of the same boys we've known our whole lives."

Zoey grimaces. "I'm sorry."

"You've done it before," I say. "Not exactly like that, but you and Luna both try to be these bigger, flashier versions of yourselves around the guys now."

She squirms. "I didn't think we were doing that."

"Well, you were."

We sit in uncomfortable silence for a minute.

"It made me feel really left out, like you and Luna were going to decide we had nothing in common and you'd bail on me." It's not pleasant to say it, but it's true.

I guess if this is the beginning of the end, there's no harm in being fully honest.

"I never actually liked Archie," I say.

I pictured what this moment would be like—or, should I

say, I've had nightmares about what this moment might be like. Me finally admitting that everything I've told Zoey over the last two months has been a lie. I pictured the way I'd be crying during it, and the way Zoey would react. Maybe she'd roll her eyes at me and say *of course* I was making the whole thing up—only someone who is as immature as me would lie about something like this. Or maybe she'd tell me that it was no big deal, that we were fine, except we'd both know that it wasn't actually fine and we'd continue to just slowly drift apart.

Either way, I didn't picture myself feeling so completely and utterly *relieved* when I came clean.

I had some practice sharing my experiment with Archie, which makes it easier to repeat it to Zoey. I tell her about my plan, about my awful attempt at flirting, and about the way I tried to kiss Archie yesterday. I don't tell her about our conversation after that, but I also tell her something I didn't tell Archie.

I tell her about Thanksgiving. About the way I watched Marcus and Brighton together and how it made me realize that I wanted to experience that feeling too. I tell her about being lonely, and that's the first time I say it out loud, but it's true. I tell her about this weird, new loneliness that I never even knew existed, and how I feel it when I watch her talk to Liam or when I see Luna and Blake holding hands when they're walking between classes.

I tell her so much that by the time I'm finished telling her all of it there are tears in my eyes. I don't know if it's from the feeling of freedom in my chest or from the fact that, surprise, surprise, it's actually really sad to tell someone that you've been feeling lonely for weeks.

"I didn't want to lose you and Luna," I finish. "I didn't want you two to leave me behind."

Unfortunately for both of us, Zoey's a sympathetic crier, so when she sees the first tear break away and slide down my face, it's all over for her, too.

"I would never do that," she sniffles. "The whole reason I keep talking about Liam is because I was so excited about the three of us doing more stuff together. Like, don't you ever picture it? Growing up and going to college together. Living together. Being each others' bridesmaids? I know it's kind of silly, but when I picture getting married, that's the only thing I know for sure I want. You there beside me."

Luna and Zoey used to have that conversation a lot. They'd talk about what their weddings would be like and I'd tell them what I did and didn't like about their plans. We'd watch those shows where people find wedding dresses or rate each other's weddings and we'd give our opinions as if we weren't nine years old. Zoey's right; even though I can't actually imagine the type of guy I would marry, the one constant was that Luna and Zoey would be there with me.

"You hate musical theater," Zoey says then. I open my mouth to protest, but she laughs and covers my face with her hand. "Stop! Don't even try to tell me that's not true. You and Luna both hate it. You don't get it. But when I drag you to my auditions and run all my lines with you, do you stop talking to me?"

I know where Zoey's going with this, obviously. It's very annoying when she has a point.

"No," I mutter.

"No!" she exclaims, throwing her arms out. It's very difficult to get Zoey out of monologue mode. "You buy tickets to all of my performances and you sit front row! You don't have to do the same things as me all the time for me to love you. Remember when I wanted to buy a pug from a breeder?"

"*Never* buy a pug from a breeder," I growl. I can't help it; I'm pretty sure those were my first words.

"But I didn't know that at the time!" Zoey exclaims. "Isn't that, like, the whole *point* of having friends?"

Ugh. I really, *really* hate when Zoey's right.

"What do I care whether you have a boyfriend or not?" she says. "I love you. So, stop being weird."

Zoey gets off my bed and flops herself over me in a bear hug.

"I'm not getting up until you promise you'll stop being weird," she says.

"I'll stop being weird," I say, but Zoey's arm is clotheslining me so it comes out all garbled.

"What's that?"

"I'll stop being weird!" I say again.

"Pardon me?"

"I'LL STOP BEING WEIRD!"

Zoey leans back, pretending to be offended. She puts her hand to her chest.

"You don't need to *shout* at me, Noah, jeez."

"I'm going to do a lot more than *shout* at both of you if you don't shut up."

Brighton's yell comes through our shared wall and Zoey and I both wince. One of the problems with being so close with my friends is that Brighton basically sees them as bonus younger sisters, which means she has no problem with threatening Zoey.

"Get ready for school," Zoey whispers. "You have a Luna to apologize to, and a Jessa to just, like . . . have any kind of interaction with? You shouldn't have lumped her in with us—she didn't do anything."

I don't have it in me to explain my complicated Jessa feelings before I've ingested a stack of ghost pancakes bigger than my head.

"Are you staying for breakfast?" I ask.

"Noah, don't be ridiculous. It's *Halloween*. Of course I'm staying for ghost pancakes."

29.

Things I'm Not Good At

1. Rollerblading
2. Mini golf
3. Apologizing

After my conversation with Zoey this morning, I know what I have to do. I understand that I was, maybe, possibly, a little unreasonable to my friends, and that includes Jessa.

Actually, maybe *especially* Jessa. I see that now.

But, the thing is, I'm not actually very good at apologizing to people. I mean, who likes to admit when they're wrong? The more wrong I am, the harder it is to admit it. And I was very, very wrong for wanting to ditch Jessa just because of who her mom is.

Ugh. Even thinking it sounds kind of ridiculous.

Jessa doesn't even look at me when I walk into homeroom, but I'm pretty sure she looks sad. The side of her face that I keep stealing glances at looks kind of sad, anyway. Even though I don't 100 percent know where Jessa and I stand, I still feel really bad about ghosting her all weekend. Thankfully, Mr. Cross is lecturing today, so there's not much time to chat even if we both wanted to.

Archie finds me on my way to lunch, coming up beside me as we walk down the hall.

"Are you okay?" he asks.

I shrug. "I told Zoey about the whole thing this morning," I say. "So now I get to go tell Luna everything."

"Good luck," Archie says. He squeezes my arm once we get to the cafeteria but then drifts off to go sit with his other friends. I think he does it to give me space to explain myself to Luna, but I don't really want him to do that because that means I'll have to *actually* explain myself to Luna.

I watch him walk to his table and realize that Jessa's already sitting there. She doesn't exactly look elated, but she smiles thinly at Archie as he sits down beside her.

So I've officially made things weird enough with Jessa that she doesn't want to sit with me at lunch. My stomach lurches.

"Look who's here!" Zoey says when I approach the table. "Our best friend, Noah!"

Luna rolls her eyes. "Last time I checked, best friends didn't call each other stupid just for having a boyfriend."

I know I'm supposed to be apologizing, but I still feel a twinge of annoyance at *boyfriend*. Blake wasn't Luna's boyfriend before this weekend, which means that after I ran off crying, she and Blake thought it would be a romantic idea to make it official.

"Last time *I* checked, best friends didn't tell whole groups of people about their best friend's crush on someone to try and make boys think they're cool."

Luna and I stare at each other for a while, both of us taking in what the other just said. I stand by my statement: I don't think it should have gone down like it did on Saturday. But I can kind of see Luna's point, too.

"Sorry," Luna and I grumble to each other at the same time.

Zoey assesses the two of us for a second.

"That's it?" she asks. She turns to Luna. "Y'know, we had a full-on heart-to-heart this morning. Tears were shed. And you two are fine with one measly little *sorry*?"

Luna and I both shrug. It's different between us. We don't always need to make a big production out of life the way Zoey does. It works for us.

"So, about all the stuff with Archie . . ." I start.

"She faked it! She faked all of it!" Zoey says.

I look at Zoey, unamused.

"Sorry," she says. "You know I love a good reveal."

"I know," Luna says.

"There's just so little *drama* in the everyday world!" Zoey says.

"No, I wasn't talking to you." Luna laughs. "I was talking to Noah."

I blink.

"You *knew*?"

"I mean, did I know that you had come up with some kind of elaborate plan to get Archie to like you, even though it was super obvious that you didn't like him? Yeah. I just didn't know the finer details of all of it. Like, y'know, *why*."

"Why didn't you say anything?" Zoey asks, swatting her on the arm.

"When your friend is going through whatever it is that makes her do something that wild, I feel like you just need to let it run its course," Luna says. "Besides, I only figured it out yesterday. If I'd known from the beginning, I would have called you out on it."

I laugh, relieved that I haven't lost Luna. But when I think about the fact that I gained her and Zoey back as friends today, it just reminds me that Jessa still isn't talking to me. Or that I'm not talking to her. Honestly, the details are blurry at this point.

I sneak another glance at Jessa and Archie. The two of them are laughing at something and Jessa throws her head back. Some of her hair falls out of its messy bun when she does that, and little gold strands frame her face. I lean on my hand and watch the way she talks, wishing and wishing that she were talking to me.

"Noah?" Zoey asks, snapping me out of it.

"What? Sorry," I say. What was I just saying? What were we talking about? "Uh, yeah, so anyway, I don't have a crush on anyone."

Luna looks at me for a long moment. She tilts her head.

"Don't you, though?"

Me and Zoey look at her confusedly. Didn't we just have this conversation? Didn't she *just* say that she'd figured out the whole thing anyway?

"No?" I say, but it comes out like a question. I can't help it:

242

Luna's always so sure of what she says that she could convince me of pretty much anything. "No, I made up all the stuff with Archie."

Luna gives me a funny look, but then quickly schools her face back into a neutral expression.

"Right," she says. "I must have misunderstood."

"You don't misunderstand things," I say, pointing my finger at her. "You always know exactly what's going on."

Luna holds her hands up defensively. "I only know what you tell me! And, sometimes, what you show me."

Wait, does Luna know?

When I told Archie *I-think-maybe-I'm-gay* in one quick breath yesterday, he just said *same* and made me laugh. Archie was always going to be a safe bet. But this is different. This is Luna and Zoey, and even though I don't think they'd ever friend dump me over something like that, it would still be a big difference between us. And a big difference is exactly what I've been trying to *avoid* with them over the last two months.

"I don't have a crush on anyone," I repeat. "And . . . I don't think I'm really ever going to have a crush on a boy. Like, at all."

I cover my face after I say it. I can't help it; I can't bear to watch Luna and Zoey process that information. I'd analyze every blink and twitch for the rest of my life, trying to make *sure* they still loved me.

When I finally gather the courage to creep my hands down away from my eyes, though, Zoey's right there in front of me.

"Noah," she says, "did you seriously think I'd be a *theater performer* and not be okay with gay people?"

It's the best thing I could have imagined she'd say.

"We love you," Luna says. "In case that wasn't clear."

"If you make me cry in the cafeteria on Halloween I will be *so* mad at you," I say, and Luna and Zoey laugh.

"Okay, we'll change the subject," Luna says. "To your *actual* crush?"

I roll my eyes. "How many times do I have to tell you? I've been so weird since the summer because I *don't* have a crush on anyone."

Somewhere in the back of my head, though, there's a little voice that's saying, *That's not true.*

Luna reaches across the table and takes both of my hands in hers.

"Think very, very hard about this," she says.

I think.

So far this school year, I've done a lot of obsessing. Over Archie, over my experiment, over what people might think about me at any given moment. But when I look back on the last two months, I don't see Archie or experiments or gossip.

I see Jessa waiting for me in homeroom, smiling widely.

I see Jessa in the shelter, playing with one of the kittens she's trying to convince her parents to adopt once he's old enough.

I see Jessa, and Jessa, and Jessa.

Oh.

Oh.

The way I think about Jessa all the time. The way I'm

always happier when she's around. The way that, even when she's making fun of me, I never want her to leave.

"Wait," I say. Luna starts to grin. "Wait, I like Jessa."

Zoey gasps and Luna laughs at her.

"Did you really not piece that together?" Luna asks her.

"I had no idea!" Zoey says.

"Me neither!" I say, laughing helplessly. But saying it out loud settles it, to me. It makes perfect sense. Of *course* I like Jessa. Everything I've been hoping to feel over the last two months, I've already been feeling.

"Well, you know what we have to do now, right?" I ask Luna and Zoey.

I'm met with blank stares, so I grin. "We have to *plan*."

30.

Things That Feel Much Better Than Expected

1. Fresh sheets on your bed
2. An open window on a cool day
3. A first crush

When I get home, I decide to use Halloween Magic to my benefit.

I've been thinking *a lot* about the last few weeks ever since my conversation with Lydia over the weekend. I've been thinking about how I've been feeling and who I've been feeling it around. And the thing I keep coming back to is the way Brighton's been speaking to me ever since I told her that I didn't have a crush on any boys.

She's still been my sister. She's still insulted my outfits and invaded my bedroom and blared her music even though she knows I hate it. But she's also been watching me carefully. She's been speaking to me more gently. She's been trying to make sure that I'm okay, from afar.

Even if I don't have a crush to talk to her about, I think she'll work pretty well for a first-time coming-out conversation.

Brighton's boots are in the front hallway when I get home,

and her jacket is hanging up on our railing (even though Mom tells her all the time not to do that, since she worked so hard to carve it), so I bolt upstairs and pound on her door until she opens it. She's only half wearing her costume, so she's got her Bonnie makeup on, but she's wearing sweatpants.

"That looks good," I say. It was the first time I didn't wear a costume to school. My only idea was Zombie Brylee James, and it didn't *quite* feel right to show up to school when Jessa and I aren't speaking dressed as an undead, evil version of her mother.

"I can do something quick for you right now if you want," Brighton says.

"That's okay," I say. "Thanks."

Brighton looks at me for a second, unsure.

"Okay?" she says. "Is that all you wanted? I'll be down in a second, I still need to get changed and—"

"I think I'm gay," I blurt out.

I say it so quickly and abruptly that it takes Brighton a second to process it. Once she does, though, her face lights up.

"Yeah!" she says. "Finally! I was starting to worry that I'd have to be the one to tell you, and I don't think I'm allowed to do that."

I laugh, but I also might be crying. I don't know. I think I'm feeling every emotion known to humankind all at once. If I *am* crying, it's fine, because Brighton's eyes are also suspiciously watery.

I give Brighton a hug, squishing my face into her tightly.

I think we'd both probably let this become the world's

longest hug, but our doorbell rings and Bonnie and Clyde let out matching screeches.

"Oh man, already?" Brighton pulls away and checks the time on her phone. "The early kids are extra early this year."

"You finish getting ready," I say. "I'll go downstairs and start handing out candy, and then you can give Bonnie and Clyde their pills."

"Ugh, gross. I'm only doing that because I have the Halloween spirit."

"So, did you figure out all your stuff from the weekend?"

Brighton asks the question once we've been sitting down together for a while, side by side on our front porch with a massive bowl of candy at our feet. We've only had a few really little kids come by so far, but they've more than delivered on the cute front.

I half nod, half shrug. "Sort of. I mean, Luna and Zoey and I are good now, but I think I might have messed things up with Jessa."

Brighton bobs her head for a second, chewing that over.

"Can I ask you something?" she asks eventually. I nod. "What do you think it was that upset you so much about Jessa?"

I've been thinking about that a lot since my conversation with Lydia, so I'm glad Brighton asked.

"I sometimes feel like I'm more attached to people than

248

they are to me," I say. "Like, do you remember my friend Kendal from a few years ago?"

Brighton snorts. "You mean the girl you had a *gigantic* baby crush on? Yeah, I seem to recall."

I blink. "That . . . makes a lot of sense, in hindsight."

"That's what I'm here for."

"But either way, I scared her off. I liked her too much. Way more than she liked me. And it made me feel like that's how everyone thought. Like if I shared my feelings or got too close to someone, they'd think I was being weird. But then when I found out that Jessa had been keeping this huge secret from me—like, she literally didn't even feel like she could invite me to her house because she saw me as this out-of-control brat who'd spit in her mom's face or something—I realized that the problem with keeping people at a distance is that people start to do it back to you. And at first, I thought I was just mad because I don't like Brylee's show, but actually it was more that I was mad at myself for being such a crappy friend."

Brighton listens to everything I say. I didn't realize how rare that was until I heard other people in school talk about how their siblings never listen to them. Brighton's always listened to what I have to say. Even if she doesn't agree with it. Even if she thinks it's silly. And even now, when I'm sure I barely made any sense. She listens, and she only responds after she's really thought about it.

"Jessa isn't like Kendal, though," she says.

"No," I agree.

"Like, Kendal didn't like you back and then got weird about it."

"Well, it's not *totally* the same," I argue. "Because . . . sorry, what?"

Kendal didn't like you back.

"Kendal didn't like me *back*?" I ask. "As in *Jessa does*?"

"I tried to talk about it with you!" Brighton says. "I figured it out on Halloween decorating day when I noticed how obsessed you two are with each other."

"Obsessed with *each other*?" I yell, which makes the couple with their toddler dressed up as a tiny firefighter stop on their way up to our porch.

Brighton and I give them matching *we're normal* smiles, and they decide to risk it by walking up the rest of the path. I hand the little girl extra candy to make up for the fact that they just witnessed me having a minor breakdown.

"What do you mean we're obsessed with each other?" I demand, whisper-yelling at Brighton once the family moves on to the next house.

Oh man, okay, I get it now. I get why Luna and Zoey were so obsessed with analyzing every interaction with Blake and Liam. *This* is how they've been feeling the entire time? How do they get anything done?

"I don't know," Brighton says. "All I'll say is that she seemed just as happy to hang out with you as you were to be hanging out with her."

"But what does that *mean*?" I drag both of my hands down my face in agony. What's the point of having an older sister who

250

already understands crushes and relationships and all of that stuff if she's not actually going to tell me all the answers?

"You should ask her that yourself," Brighton says.

I laugh, but then I realize she's serious.

"Uh, no," I say. "She doesn't even want to talk to me right now. And besides, how would that conversation even go? *Hey Jessa, sorry I was a butthead to you earlier. Anyway, wanna kiss now?*"

"I mean, it could use some fine-tuning, but it's not awful." Brighton shrugs. "And anyway, I meant that you should ask her yourself because she's walking down our street right now."

Panicked, I look out to the road that's starting to fill up with trick-or-treaters to find Luna, Zoey, Archie, Blake, and Jessa quickly approaching.

Oh no. We always, always, *always* trick-or-treat together.

"This might be the last year it's socially acceptable for me to do this, and, by god, I'm going to milk it for everything it's worth," Zoey shouts once the group is in our front yard. Jessa still isn't looking at me, so I don't look at her. That's probably for the best. I think if I looked at her for too long right now my face would catch on fire.

Brighton leans back on the porch steps. "Go get your girl," she says, drawing out *girl* into a mortifying drawl.

"Oh my god, shut up," I hiss. None of my friends say anything, so either they didn't hear what Brighton said or they didn't get it, but still. There's no need for her to torture me like that. I have the whole *torturing Noah* thing covered.

31.

Things That Are Less Scary Than Expected

1. Jumping in a lake at the beginning of the season
2. Giving six pugs heartworm medication
3. First kisses

When I fall in line with the group, Luna and Zoey each take one of my arms and squeeze. They don't even know what Brighton and I were talking about just now, but I must have a dazed look on my face if both of them think I need comfort. Having their support makes me walk a little taller as we hit the first couple of houses, even though Jessa is still ignoring me, walking closely alongside Archie.

By the time we're three houses in, though, I turn around after collecting my candy to see Blake standing right behind me, shuffling from foot to foot.

"Can I talk to you?" he asks. I nod, so the two of us hang back as everyone else goes to the next house. It's dark now, the air smells like bonfires, and the sound of everyone having fun and running around outside lifts my spirits.

"I'm sorry," Blake says. We're standing in the road like we're the parents of our group, which is funny since now I'm pretty sure I'm never going to do that with a guy for real. I almost laugh, a bit hysterically, at that thought.

I shrug. "I know about Archie now," I say. "So it's fine."

"No, it's not fine!" Blake says. He looks genuinely distressed. "I didn't know not everyone knew about Archie. *And the way I phrased it was so bad.* Sometimes I say things without thinking and people get mad at me. Like, I'm glad you know what I meant, but it still sucks that you thought I was saying you were ugly or whatever."

I'm about to respond, but Blake seems to be on a roll now. "Because you aren't ugly! Or, I mean, like. I think Luna's the prettiest, obviously. But I don't just like her because she's pretty! I—"

"Blake." I put him out of his misery. "It's fine. Really. Thanks for apologizing."

I think he worked up a sweat after all that. He seems extremely relieved that I'm not mad at him, which is pretty sweet. He trots off to go meet Luna a little ways down the road, and then we all get sucked into the trick-or-treating haze.

By the time some of the houses have started to run out of candy and our pillowcases are almost to the point of overflowing, we've circled most of the neighborhood and convene back at my house.

Tradition states that everyone comes inside and we all sort and trade our candy together. But I don't know if everyone in this group wants to hang out with me for longer than absolutely necessary.

"Are you guys coming in?" I ask, hating the way I'm actually not sure what the answer will be. Archie nudges Jessa forward, and everyone starts walking up my front yard toward my parents.

"How'd you guys make out?" my mom asks, in a full face of special-effects makeup that has definitely traumatized at least one small child tonight.

"We're gonna eat like kings!" Zoey says, hoisting her pillowcase full of candy over her head.

We all clamber up to my room, where bags of candy are dumped out and everyone begins haggling.

"I'll be right back," Jessa says. My heart leaps into my throat because that's the first thing she's said to me all night. I mean, she didn't actually say it to *me*, but it's the closest we've gotten. "Just going to the bathroom."

She gets up, and my eyes follow her out the door. She shuts it behind her and I allow myself one private little sigh.

That is, until I look away from the door and realize it might not have been so private, since every single other person is staring at me.

Luna's grinning, looking back and forth between the door and me.

"Oh yeah?" I ask, frustrated. "Do you think this is going *well*?"

"Wait," Archie says. "Did you figure it out?"

I groan, burying my face in my hands.

"You knew too?" I demand.

"I've known pretty much the whole time," he says. "Or, I mean, I had a pretty decent guess."

"Why didn't any of you *tell me*?"

"I figured you'd eventually work it out," Archie says. "It felt like something you needed to figure out by yourself."

"Uh, hi," Blake says, raising his hand like we're in class. "I didn't know. I still don't know. What are we talking about?"

"Noah likes Jessa!" Zoey says, and then slaps both hands over her mouth, looking at me with wide eyes.

She's probably worried that we're about to have a repeat of the Saturday situation on our hands, but I don't feel any of the fear or anger that I felt that day. Sure, maybe if Zoey had said that in front of the whole school, or my parents or something, I wouldn't be happy, but she wouldn't do that. Here, where it's just my friends, it's honestly kind of nice. It feels so much better to hear Zoey say that I like Jessa, rather than the twisty gut feeling I kept having when someone brought up Archie for the last couple of months. This just seems right.

I don't have to pretend. I don't have to analyze. I can say whatever comes to my head and I know that, even if not everyone in the room understands it, they'll still understand *me*.

It's different from how it used to be, but it's not bad. The deep-down stuff is still the same.

"Oh," Blake says. He looks at me for a second. "That makes a lot more sense than you liking Archie."

Luna pats him on the arm like *congrats on figuring that out, buddy* and I snort.

"So does Jessa like you?" Blake asks.

My shoulders slump. That's the part that I've been trying not to think about.

"I don't know," I say. "My sister said she thought she might, but also Jessa hasn't spoken to me all night."

"You need to talk to her," Zoey says. "Tonight! Tell her how you feel!"

Sometimes, I think that Zoey thinks every day is just one big audition for a teen drama show.

"And also probably apologize?" Luna says. "Y'know, for the whole not-speaking-to-her-for-several-days situation?"

"Yes, thank you," I say. "I needed the reminder. It's not like that's the only thought I've had all day or anything."

If Jessa actually does like me back, I think I might grow wings and fly away. If she's thinking all the things that I'm thinking, if she wants to spend all her time with me, if she wants me to be that person for her? It would be the best thing ever. But also if Jessa actually *does* like me back, that means I actually have to *do something* about it.

"Why's it so quiet in here?" Jessa asks, opening the door and sending a jolt through me. She sits down behind her candy pile. "I thought one of you might've killed all the others for first candy dibs or something."

"We would never do that," Luna says automatically. "We have a system."

"Anyway!" Zoey chirps. "Now I need to go to the bathroom. Luna, can you help me?"

"Ew, what?" Luna wrinkles her nose, but then Zoey gives her a look and she says, "Oh! Yes, of course."

The two of them race out of the room together.

"Uh, I need to talk to your dad about . . . puberty," Blake says. He stands up and looks down at Archie meaningfully.

Archie looks at him for a second, like *THAT was the best you could come up with?*

"Me too, I guess." He sighs, standing up, and then it's just me and Jessa in the room together.

She still can't quite look at me, and I feel so awful that I caused this. Jessa's the one who had to start everything over at a new school. I was supposed to be the person who made that easier, and instead I'm the person who can't seem to stop making her life more complicated.

"I'm really sorry," I say. I don't think there's anything else I can really say yet. The rest doesn't matter if Jessa doesn't want to forgive me.

Jessa finally, *finally* looks at me, and my stomach flips. Has it always done that when we make eye contact? I think maybe, but I didn't know what it meant.

"For what?" she asks. "I genuinely don't even know what I did so wrong."

I gulp and try not to panic. If Jessa hates me after this, then I'll just have to deal with that.

"I saw you walking out of your house on Saturday night," I say. "And I recognized it from the Brylee special we watched. Brylee James is your *mom*, and you never told me. And at first,

I was *so* upset. I was really mad at you for not telling me earlier. I was basically blaming you for everything I hate about *Rural Refresh*, which I know is ridiculous."

"*Extremely* ridiculous," Jessa says, crossing her arms.

"And I'm sorry for being so mean about her," I say. "Your mom, I mean. I'm sure she's not actually that bad."

"*The devil in pink coveralls* I believe was the name you've used for her most recently."

I wince. "It's not fair of me to put all of my issues with *Rural Refresh* onto you, and it's also not fair for me to put all of my issues with Middletown getting busier onto your mom."

"Not liking a TV show isn't a reason to act like you did." She looks away from me again and I want to shout, *No, come back!*

"It definitely, *definitely* isn't," I agree. "But I eventually realized I was upset because you didn't feel like you could tell me. I was worried that you didn't like me as much as I like you."

That gets Jessa's attention. She eyes me carefully.

"How much is that?" she asks.

I can see that tiny glimmer of hope in Jessa's eyes, and it makes my whole heart light up. I take a shaky breath in and out.

"That I didn't need to force myself to have a crush on Archie," I say, very quietly. "Because I had one on you the whole time."

A shocked little giggle escapes Jessa's mouth.

"Really?" she asks, as if I didn't just bare my entire soul for her.

"Yes, really." I laugh. "Obviously."

"No, no!" Jessa wags her finger in my face. "Not *obviously*! Not obviously, when I've liked you since *camp* and I had to watch you agonize over Archie! There was nothing *obvious* about that situation!"

I cover my face with my hands and laugh. "Stop! That's so embarrassing."

I say it, but I don't really feel embarrassed. I'm mostly freaking out at the fact that Jessa just said she's liked me *since camp*. The whole time!

My hands are still over my eyes when Jessa takes them in hers and lowers them. We look at each other for a second.

Jessa leans forward. I lean forward. Our lips meet in the middle, just for a second. Just long enough for me to feel how soft Jessa's lips are and to make my stomach flip-flop-flip-flop so quickly it's like I'm bungee jumping.

When Jessa leans back, both of us laugh. I've thought so much about having a first kiss that I never really considered what happens *after*. How am I supposed to have a normal conversation with her, now that I know that she likes me and I think (okay, I know) that I want to kiss her again?

But then Jessa says, "Do you think Blake's really asking your dad about puberty?"

And it's just like it's always been. Both of us laugh (I'm maybe a bit extra loud because I can't believe what just happened), and I'm suddenly so happy that there's a group of people downstairs who are going to want to ask us a million questions.

Because even if it's annoying, it means they care.

"I guess we should go find out," I say, even though I'd much rather stay right here in this moment with Jessa forever.

"I guess we'd better," Jessa agrees.

Just before we get to the door, she takes my hand. I look down at our fingers as they interlace and lock into place.

Maybe not *all* change is bad.

Acknowledgments

Noah isn't for everyone. She's prickly, and insecure, and impulsive, and if you've read this whole book then I'm sure you've said "Why is she *doing that*?" more than once.

But, of everything I've ever written, Noah is the character most like me. Figuring out what made her tick helped me figure it out for myself. If you know her, if you love her, if you are her: thank you for being exactly the way you are.

Thank you to my agent, Claire Friedman, for, uh, all of this. You're the best of the best of the best, but if you're reading this please take a nap.

Thank you to Lily Kessinger, Noah's first fan, for being willing to take a leap on a girl so in-progress. Thank you to Elizabeth Agyemang for working tirelessly to shape this book to become the best it could be. Thank you to Lucy Zhang, my cover artist, and Jessie Gang, my designer, for so perfectly capturing Noah on the cover, and Megan Gendell and Emily Andrukaitis for making her shine on the inside. Huge thank-yous, always, to the rest of my Harper team: Samantha Brown, Melissa Cicchitelli, Emily Mannon, and Heather Tamarkin.

While I remember *very* clearly what it was like to feel the way Noah feels about love for most of this book, I somehow managed to land the most incredible wife on the planet. Gabi, I'm so glad you like me back. Thank you for being perfect and for having equally perfect babies with me.

Thank you to Rebecca Barrow and Rory Power for, let's face it, essentially having to hold my hand while I whined nonstop about how difficult this book was to write. Annoyingly, you guys were right: it turned out really well.

Possibly the coolest benefit of getting to write books is finding support in the most unexpected places. On that note, thank you to Doug McPherson, Karlo Melgar, and Robbie McCue, my accidental street team. Drinks on Noah tonight.

Finally, thank you to you, for giving Noah a shot. I'm sure she'd never admit it, but she's really glad you're here.